DESIRE

A Crown and Glory Lesbian Love Story

Zuri Amara

Lipsey & Love Legacy Press, LLC

Desire: A Crown and Glory Lesbian Love Story
by Zuri Amara

Published by Lipsey & Love Legacy Press, LLC

For inquiries, contact the publisher at:
Hello@LipseyLoveLegacyPress.com

Paperback Edition

ISBN 979-8-9942794-5-8

Published in the United States of America
10 9 8 7 6 5 4 3 2 1

PUBLISHER'S DISCLAIMER

Crown and Glory: Lesbian Love Stories of the Black Women of the Crown and Glory Natural Hair Salon is a fictional series crafted for grown, consenting adults who appreciate sensual, unapologetic storytelling. Within these pages, you'll find explicit depictions of intimacy between women—Black women loving, desiring, and cherishing each other in body and spirit.

Every character is fictional and at least 18 years old. Unless otherwise indicated, all the names, characters, businesses, places, events, and incidents in this book are either the product of the author's imagination or used in a fictitious manner. Any resemblance to actual people, living or dead, or actual events is purely coincidental.

Please read the trigger warnings listed before each book or story. If the contents may trigger unwanted emotions or memories, please do not read further. Please protect your mental health and peace of mind.

This work celebrates Black lesbian love in all its heat, humor, tenderness, and joy. It is intended for entertainment and artistic expression only, not as a manual for real-life relationships or sexual activity. Reader discretion is advised: if sexually explicit content offends you, or you are not of legal age in your jurisdiction to view such material, please close this book now.

By choosing to read on, you affirm that you are older than 18 years, are legally permitted to access adult content, and understand that the author and publisher bear no responsibility for how this fictional world may be interpreted or applied beyond the page.

THE CROWN & GLORY LESBIAN ROMANCES

A place where Black women are cherished, desired, adored, comforted, devoted, and loved. Read the stories of the women who make Crown & Glory a community.

Cherish: Dana & Abike

A guarded mechanic discovers that the woman she trusts with her locs is the one she can trust with her heart.

Adored: Bevanne & Kiah

A single mother and an accountant discover that vulnerability is the greatest act of courage.

Comfort: Dawn & Sara

A widow and a professor facing lupus find solace, faith, and unexpected love.

Desire: Celeste & Jabari

Two women chasing impossible dreams discover passion where they least expect it.

Devoted: Toni & Nia

A Navy veteran and a wedding planner decide whether they're ready for a forever kind of love.

The Salon Sisterhood

Read the Crown and Glory Series first five books, with bonus chapters, in this compilation.

Haven: Lyric & Mouse

A young stylist with a troubled past finds safety, healing, and home.

Home: Meeka & Tavia

Two women searching for belonging discover that home can be a person.

Balance: Imani & Saffron

An enemies-to-lovers romance between structure and spontaneity.

Secrets: Zee & Jasmine & Cole

A second chance at love complicated by secrets, trauma, and hard truths.

Also by Zuri Amari

Maybe More Than Friends: Sophie and Aya

Who knew that a college friendship could grow into lifetime love?

Dedication

To my clients,

Thank you for the stories, the laughter, the tears, the wisdom, and the years we shared together.

Though these women are fictional, the sisterhood of Crown & Glory was inspired by the remarkable women who crossed my path and enriched my life.

May every woman find friendship that sustains her, community that embraces her, and love that reminds her who she is.

— Zuri Amara

WELCOME TO CROWN & GLORY

Dear Reader,

The chair is ready.

The kettle is on.

We're playing smooth jazz today.

Someone is laughing too loudly in the next room. Somebody brought food that smells entirely too good. You are welcome to sample a bit before you leave. Around here, we like to share calories.

In other words, it's a normal day at Crown & Glory.

Thank you for stopping by. Whether this is your first visit to the salon or you're returning to spend time with old friends, I'm delighted you're here.

The women you'll meet in these pages aren't perfect, but they are resilient, loving, and determined to build lives filled with joy, love, purpose, and connection.

Their journeys may be different, but they all discover the same truth: life is better when we don't have to walk through it alone.

I hope this story makes you smile, keeps you turning pages long past bedtime, and leaves you feeling a little lighter than when you began.

Now get comfortable with a hot cup of tea or coffee and enjoy your appointment.

With love,

Zuri Amara

Founder of the Crown & Glory Salon Sisterhood

CONTENTS

CHAPTER 1

The Color Disaster

Celeste

Celeste knew the color was off the second she rinsed the toner.

Too brassy. Too warm. Too damn loud.

She ran a towel around the client's shoulders, trying to stay calm while her stomach did gymnastics. She'd double-checked the formula, pre-toned like she was taught, even took a photo in natural light before mixing. But somewhere between step two and panic, the shade veered from "soft honey glow" to “late summer traffic cone.”

She smiled tightly into the mirror.

“Well,” her client said, peering at herself with that polite, southern-tight smile. “It's… different.”

Celeste swallowed. “Let me grab one of the senior stylists real quick. we can tone it down just a touch.”

The woman nodded, unsure. And Celeste made her escape to the breakroom, pulse loud in her ears.

Bevanne was sipping from her “#BLACKHAIRMATTERS” mug and scrolling on her phone. Dawn leaned against the counter near the mini fridge, peeling a clementine like she had nowhere to be.

Celeste walked in, breathing like she’d just run a lap.

“I messed up,” she said.

Both stylists looked up.

“What kind of messed up?” Bevanne asked, already rising. “We talkin’ ‘it’ll grow back’ or ‘we can fix it before she posts a Yelp review’?”

“Toner’s too warm. It’s giving brass, not blonde.”

Dawn raised an eyebrow. “First toner fumble? Girl, welcome to the club. I once turned a girl’s leave-out orange. Like… *Cheez-It* orange.”

Celeste blinked. “Deadass?”

Dawn popped a clementine slice in her mouth. “Swear. Had to buy her a silk press and a smoothie to stop her from cryin’.”

Bevanne nodded, already grabbing gloves. “I had a dude come in with an itchy scalp for a wash and twist. I accidentally used clarifying shampoo with peppermint oil. His scalp lit up like the Fourth of July. Man started praying out loud in the chair.”

Celeste laughed weakly.

"You're not special, baby," Bevanne said, squeezing her shoulder. "You're new. That's all."

"I just… I wanted it to be perfect. It's my first week on the floor, and now she's out there lookin' like a candle flame."

"She alive?" Dawn asked.

"Yes."

"She cussed you out?"

"No."

"She still in the chair?"

"…Yeah."

"Then you're ahead of the curve."

Celeste followed them out, still shaken but a little steadier. She wasn't the only one who had crashed at the start. She was just the latest.

And that meant she'd survive it too.

Back at the station, Bevanne took the lead with a calm smile. "Hey, love, I hear the tone came out a bit warmer than planned. Totally fixable. I'm Bevanne, one of the senior stylists. We're just gonna cool that shade down a little."

The client relaxed immediately. Dawn leaned against the counter nearby, gently affirming everything Bevanne said with quiet nods and a reassuring presence. Celeste stood close, watching every move.

Bevanne worked with quick, practiced confidence, toning the color down on the woman's short locs using a muted ash glaze to soften the warmth. She walked Celeste through each step, not to show off, but to show her *how*.

"This happens a lot more than you'd think," she said while fingering the color through. "Coloring natural locs is different from processed hair, and locs take color differently from client to client. Sometimes the product oxidizes faster than expected. It could be porosity, the tightness of the locs, or the mood of the ancestors. Don't panic — just pivot."

After processing, they rinsed and styled the client's hair, adding a bit of oil to keep it healthy. The color wasn't perfect — not yet — but it looked intentional, stylish, and way closer to what the client originally asked for.

And more importantly, *the client was smiling.*

Bevanne crouched beside her and said, "We'll give the hair a couple of weeks to rest, then we'll do a full-tone correction, free of charge. And Celeste will be ready to take the lead next time, she's got the eye. Just needed a little backup."

The woman beamed. "Honestly, I appreciate y'all. The way you handled this? Real professional, warm. I'll definitely come back to finish the look with Celeste."

Celeste blinked, stunned. "For real?"

"Absolutely," the client said, standing. "You cared. That matters. And your mentors got you. That tells me everything I need to know."

Later, as the client left, Celeste just stood still, heart pounding, but no longer panicked.

Dawn handed her the used towel with a soft grin. "Congratulations. You officially survived your first crisis. And I bet you got a client for life. People will forgive a mistake if you are honest and don't abandon them."

Celeste let out a laugh. The kind that rises from relief and crashes into gratitude.

She'd made a mistake. She'd gotten help. And she'd been trusted with a chance to try again.

CHAPTER 2

In Charge

Jabari

Jabari stared at the wall socket for a long second, then dropped to her knees and pressed her forehead to the cool linoleum.

"Why—" she whispered, "—won't you just *work*?"

The outlet blinked back in silence.

She'd just spent thirty minutes assembling a shelf meant for toddler shoes, only to realize she didn't have enough screws. The sink she'd ordered for the infants' room was still boxed in the middle of the hallway because no one had brought a dolly. She sure wasn't paying another $80 for delivery labor. She'd planned to move it herself until she realized it weighed more than she could lift.

And the electricians, who were supposed to be done *last Friday*, had halfway installed the outlets, left wires hanging out, re-wired a light switch *backwards*, and then ghosted after cashing the deposit. She'd left voicemails. Emails. She even found one of them on Instagram and DM'd him, as if she were begging for a situationship closure. With the half-assed electrical job, she couldn't legally plug in the fridge for breast milk or juice boxes, *one of the dozens of regulations* tied to their city opening permit.

Jabari sat back on her heels and took a deep breath. The familiar itch of panic started under her skin. The therapist at UNC Charlotte had her practice this in a mock child development class when her perfectionism flared up. It didn't always work, but today, it was all she had.

She pressed a hand to her chest and tried to remember what the therapist at UNC Charlotte had said:

"Breathe in. Breathe out. Name what you can control."

She could control… the fact that she had made a checklist. And a backup checklist.

She could control… the fact that she brought her drill, tools, and measuring tape.

She could control… her breath. Maybe.

The door at the front of the daycare space squeaked as her student, Solomon, walked past with boxes of shelves for the infants' room. Jabari waved, her face composed, her eyes dry. No one needed to see the chaos behind her eyes. Especially not the undergrad assigned to her for course credit. There was no "panicked and crying in the supply closet" checkbox on their rubric. Which, for the record, she *had* done earlier that morning.

Abike had so much faith in her. She had said, *"You're smart, you're organized, and you care. That's the whole job, Jabari."*

But faith wasn't insulation. It didn't keep the ductwork from sagging. It didn't fast-track city daycare permits, schedule inspections for this decade, or chase down contractors who'd ghosted after cashing the deposit.

She stood slowly and wiped her palms on her pants. She hadn't eaten since breakfast, and her stomach was starting to remind her that granola bars and coffee were not food, not really.

The thought of her ex popped into her head uninvited. Lamont would always lecture her about *trying to do too much.* Said it *wasn't "ladylike" to boss people around like she was in charge.* But he didn't live here anymore, and he sure as hell wasn't the one under this kind of pressure. He wasn't the one holding a grant-funded dream together with duct tape and student labor. And he certainly wasn't the one staying up till 2 a.m. researching building codes on a tablet with a cracked screen.

Besides, she *was* in charge.

CHAPTER 3

Out Back

Celeste

The salon buzzed on without her.

Inside, blow dryers roared, laughter rang out, and Afrobeats bounced from the Bluetooth speaker someone had finally connected to the internet.

Celeste slipped out the back door, fingers trembling as she fumbled with her phone. She needed air. Space. Something that wasn't warm lighting and women who made it all look so damn easy.

She pressed her back against the brick wall, exhaled too hard, then bent at the waist, hands on her knees. Her heart wouldn't slow down. Her brain wouldn't shut up.

You really thought you were ready? Thought you'd come outta school and slay every head? Please.

She sat down hard on the edge of the concrete ramp, knees up, arms folded tight over them. Her hands were still faintly stained from dye, and her sneakers were dusty from the gravel lot where she'd tried, and failed, to get her car to start at lunch.

That 2009 Sentra had wheezed, blinked, and gone quiet. No turnover. No click. Just a whine and a check engine light she'd been ignoring for two weeks. She'd called it a fluke and walked back inside. But she knew what it meant.

She didn't have the money for repairs. Hell, she didn't have enough for an oil change *and* groceries.

Charlotte might be a "big city" in the South, but it wasn't New York. There was no train she could hop. No buses running every six minutes. If your car broke down in Charlotte, you were out of luck, stranded, both professionally and personally.

She dropped her phone in her lap. Battery 1%. No missed calls. No miracles. Almost no charge.

And suddenly the tears came fast, hot, too loud in her ears. She covered her face with both hands, but it didn't stop the sound.

She hated herself for crying like a little kid. But right now? That's exactly how she felt.

Like a broke, tired, embarrassed, defeated little girl who had no idea what she was doing.

It wasn't just the coloring mistake. It wasn't just the car. It wasn't just the broke-as-hell bank account or the mountain of student loans about to hit.

It was the crushing feeling that she was ***failing*** before she even had a chance to shine.

She'd fought hard to be here. She'd left New York. She'd passed the damn boards. She got into Crown and Glory, *the* Crown and Glory, and still... here she was. Sobbing behind a building like a cautionary tale.

"Life is *life-ing* all over me," she muttered to herself, voice ragged.

She felt like she couldn't breathe.

She felt like she couldn't *handle it.*

Then, the soft click of the back door opening.

Footsteps. Slower. Hesitant.

Celeste didn't look up.

Jabari

Jabari grabbed her clipboard, stuffed an energy bar in her mouth, and stepped outside.

The back alley behind the salon was a quiet strip of cracked pavement between the daycare's back door and the side entrance to Crown and Glory. Heat shimmered off the concrete. The only thing moving was her own damn anxiety.

She leaned against the ramp railing and let her eyes close for a second.

That's when she saw *her.*

A woman, short with a pulled-back natural Afro-puff, sitting on the low concrete step like the sidewalk had tackled her. Shoulders tight. Hands over her face. Rocking slightly and talking to herself.

And crying.

Not a cute, single tear. Real crying. Messy, private, unraveling sobs.

Jabari froze.

She didn't know what to do. Her default was efficiency, not emotional rescue. But something in her body moved before her mind could veto it.

"Uh… you okay?"

The woman looked up, red-eyed, breathing hard. "Yeah. I mean… no. Not really."

Jabari exhaled. "Same."

The words were out before she could second-guess them.
They introduced themselves. Celeste. A stylist. Brooklyn accent and tear-streaked cheeks. Cute even through stress.

She'd messed up a client's color. Her car was dead. She didn't know how she was going to pay for repairs. And everything felt like too much.

The more Celeste talked, the more Jabari recognized the look, the weight, the spiral, the ache of disappointment with yourself before the world even gets to judge you.

When Celeste started crying again, Jabari didn't think. She just moved.

Arm around shoulders. Light pressure. Not too much. Just enough to say: *I got you. Right now, I got you.*

She'd spent the last week trying to hold everything together. Make decisions. Look confident. Feel nothing. But this-this right here was real. Messy. Raw. Honest.

Celeste was worried about her car. Jabari was worried about a six-figure facility that might not open on time. But pain was painful. Panic was scary. And relief was appreciated, no matter where it came from.

They weren't friends. Not yet. But this? Two Black women, standing behind a building, both quietly falling apart, yet trying to hold each other up without judgment.

This was real.

When Celeste laughed through her tears, Jabari laughed too.

Jabari blinked. "You want me to call someone for you?"

"I was gonna call Dana. She said if I ever needed anything with the car..."

"Dana, as in Abike's wife? Vintage car lady?"

"Yeah. She's cool." Celeste wiped her cheeks. "And also terrifying."

"Terrifying but dependable. Good combo," Jabari said, pulling out her phone. "Here, you talk. I've got full bars, and it is charged."

Celeste gave a watery laugh and took the phone. Dana answered on the second ring.

"Y'all better not be calling me with another busted alternator," Dana barked.

Celeste grimaced. "It's Celeste. Sorry. My car's dead. No noise. No click. Just vibes."

"Where you at?"

"Out back of the salon."

"I'll be there in twenty."

Jabari took the phone and gave her a gentle smile. "See? You're not alone."

Celeste looked down at her chipped nails and dusty shoes and swallowed hard. "Thanks."

Jabari shrugged. "I get it. We're all out here trying to keep it together. It's okay to fall apart a little."

Celeste nudged her shoulder lightly. "You're kinda good at this pep talk thing."

"I majored in early childhood development. Toddlers taught me how to keep folks from melting down." Jabari smirked. "You're just a slightly taller toddler with a killer twist-out."

Celeste smiled for real this time. Not everything was fixed. Her car still wasn't running, her money was still funny, and tomorrow was another long shift. But for this one moment, she didn't feel like she was drowning.

Jabari

Celeste smiled, and something inside Jabari softened. *There she is*, she thought. *There's the girl underneath the panic.* And maybe, just maybe, that girl wasn't the only one who needed saving today.

And for the first time in weeks, Jabari didn't check her email. Didn't text a contractor. Didn't touch her clipboard. She just sat beside someone who saw her. Not as "the manager." Not as "Abike's hire." Just a woman. A mess. And still worthy of care. Arm around her shoulders. Light pressure. Not too tight. Just *presence*.

Celeste leaned in. And Jabari exhaled for the first time all day.

Something resonated in the middle of all the mess, the brass-colored regret, the busted car, the paper-thin finances.

Not fixed. Not solved.

But held.

Just when the silence started to settle, a low rumble rolled into the alley; steady, powerful, unmistakable. A gleaming, red '76 Chevy, engine rumbling like thunder, pulled up. The vintage pickup truck backed smoothly into the lot, its paint job gleaming like it had been waxed by hand and blessed by ancestors. The door swung open, revealing a tall, muscular woman in coveralls, wearing Aviator shades, her locs pulled back, and her expression flat like traffic court on a Monday. She stepped out in ripped jeans and a sleeveless tee that read *STAY GREASY* across the chest.

Dana.

Celeste recognized her immediately. Abike's wife. The one who ran that auto restoration shop off Statesville Ave. She was practically a legend. Half the stylists swore by her. They claimed she could diagnose a busted engine just by hearing it cough.

Celeste blinked. "Is she… in a Fast & Furious spin-off I missed?"

"Probably," Jabari said with a grin.

Dana didn't wave. She just nodded once and walked straight to Celeste, taking keys already dangling from her hand like she knew the whole story.

"This is the one that won't start?"

Celeste stood, wiping her face quickly. "Yeah… she's been struggling."

Dana opened the driver's door, sat behind the wheel, and tried the ignition: a low whine, a sputter, nothing.

She popped the hood, poked around, and let out a low whistle. "Starter's fried. Battery's on life support. Alternator probably next. Who did your last oil change?"

Celeste blinked. "...God?"

Jabari stifled a laugh.

Dana closed the hood gently like she was tucking the car into hospice care. "She'll need a little love."

"I... don't know if I can afford love right now," Celeste admitted, her voice small again.

Dana shrugged. "Good thing we do family rates."

Celeste blinked. "What?"

Dana gestured between Celeste and Jabari. "Y'all part of Crown and Glory. That makes you family. I'll tow her back to the shop, do a full workup. We'll get her street safe. No labor markup. Parts at cost."

Celeste's eyes stung again, but this time it wasn't panic, it was relief so sharp it made her knees feel weak.

"You serious?"

Dana looked over, eyebrow raised. "I don't joke about cars."

Jabari grinned. "She really doesn't."

Within minutes, Dana had the car hooked up to the tow hitch like she'd done it a thousand times because she had.
Before climbing back into her truck, she gave Celeste one last look, not pitying, but serious.

"When I finish, we'll have a little talk about car maintenance. But you did the hard part. You asked for help. That was a responsible decision, grown."

Celeste nodded, too choked up to speak.

"Check in tomorrow. I'll know more after I run diagnostics."

And with that, Dana pulled off, one woman, one busted car, and one less weight on Celeste's shoulders.

Celeste and Jabari stood side by side in the fading afternoon heat, watching Dana's truck disappear around the corner, hauling Celeste's busted car like it weighed nothing.

Neither of them spoke for a second.

Then Celeste let out a sharp exhale and shook her head. "I'm glad Dana thinks I'm grown."

Jabari cracked up. "That's the highest possible praise. Dana doesn't hand out compliments unless you bleed for 'em."

Celeste smiled, and for the first time all day, it didn't feel like it might crack under the weight of everything.

They were quiet for another beat — not awkward, not intense. Just calm. The kind of calm that shows up *after* a storm.

Jabari tilted her head. "Hey… I can give you a ride home if you want. I'll be here for a while; I still have some cleanup and student check-ins to finish. But just let me know when you're ready."

Celeste looked over, surprised but touched. "Thank you. For real."

They pulled out their phones and exchanged numbers, fingers moving slower than usual, like neither of them wanted to rush past the moment.

"Alright," Jabari said. "Go finish being brilliant. I'll text when I'm wrapping up."

Celeste smirked. "Brilliant feels a little outta reach today, but I'll settle for 'still standing.'"

Jabari nodded. "Same."

They stood like that for a while, breathing easier in each other's presence, until the door creaked again behind them and the world reminded them to get back to it.

But now, at least, they knew they weren't the only ones struggling to hold it all together. That counted for something.

And with that, they parted, each walking back into their own chaos, but a little lighter. A little steadier. A little *less alone*.

CHAPTER 4

We Got You

Celeste

Inside the salon, Crown and Glory was humming the way it always did: low chatter, clinking bobby pins, soft R&B sliding through the speakers like honey on toast.

Celeste sat in the break room, clutching a cold bottle of water and trying not to feel like a child in time-out.

Bevanne was across from her, unwrapping foil from her sandwich, giving side-eyes like they were hugs. "So what exactly happened, baby girl?"

Celeste sighed. "Color was off. Not terrible, but not what she wanted. I rushed through the toner 'cause I was nervous and trying to stay on time. Then my car wouldn't start, and" Her voice cracked. "It just felt like... everything."

Dawn leaned against the doorframe, arms crossed over her vintage overalls. "Lemme guess, you thought you were supposed to glide outta beauty school with angel hands and flawless timing?"

Celeste nodded weakly.

"Chile," Dawn said, taking a loud bite of her plantain chips, "I once dyed a woman's hair *green* by accident. She was trying to go silver-blonde. I had to pretend like it was an edgy fashion choice just so she wouldn't cry in the chair."

Bevanne snorted. "She wore a beanie for two weeks."

Celeste let out a small laugh, grateful and ashamed at once.

Bevanne reached over and touched her hand. "It's called learning. You'll do it every day for the rest of your life if you're lucky."

"Everybody gets bruised," Dawn added. "The trick is not lettin' a bruise turn into a scar. Understand?"

Celeste nodded again, throat tight.

"Now," Bevanne said, "Did I hear Dana's truck out back?"
"Yeah. Jabari called her for me."

"See?" Dawn winked. "Already got salon magic working in your favor."

Celeste tried to smile. It helped. Not everything was fixed. But the weight didn't feel quite so heavy with hands holding it beside her.

Jabari

Game Plans and Sisterhoods

Jabari sipped lukewarm coffee from a paper cup and squinted at the portable sink like it had insulted her ancestors.

It still sat dead-center in the hallway, taped-up box, top flopped open like a wound. The dolly hadn't materialized, and neither had a volunteer strong enough to move it solo.

But she had Solomon, a freshman majoring in early childhood education from Johnson C. Smith University (JCSU). He was eager, respectful, and chronically underestimating the weight of things. Jabari liked him.

"So, here's the play," she said, flipping open her clipboard. "We cut the box open where it is, extract the parts, carry them in pieces to the infant room, and assemble in place."

Solomon nodded solemnly. "Taking what the offense gives us."

Jabari smiled. "Exactly."

"And then you're hitting City Hall in the morning?"

"First thing. Face to face. I've sent five emails and left more voicemails. We're way past emails and voicemails now. I'll go to the electrician's office, too. You can work on those short shelves for the children's cubbies."

Solomon grinned and picked up a box cutter. "You're teaching me so much, Ms. Jabari. This is why you get paid the big bucks."

Jabari let out a short, dry laugh. "If only."

Still, she appreciated the compliment. It felt... grounding.

"Careful with that box cutter. An ER visit is not on our schedule." As Solomon sliced open the box and started organizing parts, Jabari crouched beside him and got to work. They worked quietly but efficiently, the way people do when they've hit the edge and decided to climb anyway. Jabari's back ached, and she was sure she had sweat stains down to her waistband, but for the first time that day, the *doing* calmed her. No waiting on contractors. No city red tape. Just her hands, her brain, and her will.

By the time they clicked the last hose into place and tested the faucet, she and Solomon exchanged a high-five with the joy of a minor victory.

She hadn't learned any of this in school.

Not how to juggle contractors who vanished mid-job. Not how to patch drywall after a delivery guy gouged it with a cart. Not how to keep smiling when your brain was spinning like a hard drive about to crash.

She learned by watching her mother stretch grocery budgets with surgical precision, and by observing her grandmother negotiate rent extensions with a casserole to the landlord.

They didn't complain. They adapted. They *pivoted* before pivoting was corporate lingo. They did the impossible with grace and leftovers.

And now here she was, not following in their footsteps so much as freestyling in the same tradition.

Celeste

Celeste ended her day like she had something to prove, not because anyone asked her to, but because that's what you did when people had your back.

She swept the entire salon floor, clearing coils and curls from under chairs and corners. Tied up the trash. Tossed used towels into the washing machine in the back, then moved dry ones from the dryer to a rolling basket and folded each one neatly. Stack after stack of soft, white cotton, ready for tomorrow.

In the storage closet, she straightened the product shelves, took stock of oils and edge gels, and retrieved the clipboard where Abike tracked the monthly orders. The detangling spray was getting low. They'd need more gloves, too. She jotted it down in careful print, her handwriting a little messier than she liked.

The shop had already quieted. Bevanne had dipped out early for dinner with her wife. Dawn had said goodnight with a "Don't work too hard, baby stylist," and a wink.

Now it was just Celeste, moving through the space with a kind of quiet gratitude. Her salon sisters had wrapped her in support earlier, with no judgment and no ego. Just love. She'd do anything for them.

And maybe she *wasn't* perfect. But she was learning.

And she *belonged* here.

She walked past the front desk to grab her bag, catching a glimpse of herself in the mirror. She paused.

Then reached up to re-twist her Afro puff, tight and high, exactly how she liked it. She brushed her teeth and slicked on a fresh layer of gloss, too, even though it was just for a ride home.

Just in case.

Because Jabari? Was *really* cute. In that smooth, quiet, get-things-done way. Like a woman who read architectural plans, drank tea with honey, and knew where all her daycare children's birth certificates were.

By the time her phone buzzed, she was all wrapped up. *Ready when you are.* She was already at the door, keys in hand, with fresh lip gloss.

She texted back: *On my way.*

CHAPTER 5

City Hall

Jabari

When morning came, Jabari was already two sips into her coffee, hair in a bun, clipboard freshly stocked with forms and backup forms. Today, she was not waiting for emails that never came. Today, she was *walking in.* The City Hall building was older than it looked online, all beige walls and buzzed-in doors, with that strange, government smell that clung to paperwork and aging carpet. Every surface gleamed a little too much from years of being wiped down by worry and bleach.

Jabari held her coffee and a folder she couldn't afford to lose.

As she waited in line at the Zoning and Inspection counter, she thought back to the night before, pulling up in front of Celeste's apartment.

It was a laid-back little spot in an older complex just off Beatties Ford Road. Vinyl siding. Balcony herb garden. A folding chair on the porch that looked well-used.

Inside had been cool and clean, with pops of personality, album covers, bold throw pillows, a candle that smelled like sage and citrus. Celeste had kicked off her sneakers the moment she walked in and offered Jabari a bottle of water like they'd done this a hundred times.

They'd sat for a bit, not long, just enough to exhale. Just enough for Celeste to say, "That plan of yours, hitting City Hall and tracking down the contractor, kinda badass."

Jabari had laughed. "I have to go old school, IRL. These people have ignored emails and ghosted my voicemails. I've been transferred so many times I ended up talking to some guy in the *morgue*."

Celeste had cackled, high and clear. "You have *got* to be kidding."

"I wish I were."

They'd both promised to stay in touch. And Jabari had meant it.

Now, standing under harsh fluorescent lights, Jabari introduced herself for the fifth time that morning.

"I'm working on the new childcare space, Children of the Dream. We got the community startup grant from the city, it's connected to Crown and Glory Salon off of Sugar Creek Road?"

The zoning clerk, mid-50s, tired eyes, red glasses, gave a tight-lipped smile and handed her a laminated checklist without looking up. "All the required forms are on the back. Next."

That was how the day started.

Smiles. Shrugs. More lines. Another hallway.

But Jabari *didn't back down.* She straightened her shoulders, sharpened her questions, and leaned in. Every 'no' got her one step closer to the 'yes' she needed.

Up in the City Planning Department, she met a woman with salt-and-pepper braids, earth-toned skin, wooden hoop earrings, and a worn UNC Charlotte lanyard around her neck. Her name tag read "Katrina."

Katrina glanced at Jabari's forms, then paused. "You're Jabari Henderson? With the Dream grant?"

"Yes!" Jabari said, her breath catching, "That's me."

Katrina's whole face shifted from neutral to something like pride. "I've heard about this project. My niece goes to JCSU. They've been bragging about this grant for weeks now."

Katrina lowered her voice, "You want to go to desk #14 next. Ask for Marlene. Tell her you already spoke to me. And whatever you do, don't let *anyone* send you back to Permits. You're already too far in. Marlene will walk you through the next steps and explain some of the fine print on those forms."

Jabari blinked. "Thank you. Seriously."

Katrina leaned in and whispered, "And avoid Mr. Slate, desk #20. If he touches your paperwork, you'll be waiting until next year. He dislikes community grants and attempts to sabotage them. It's political for him."

Jabari tucked that name away. *Mr. Slate = Hell no.*

By noon, she had a folder packed with notes and printed checklists, but this time, they had annotations in the margins. She had three new business cards. A direct cell number for a city liaison. And an in-person appointment next week with an electrical inspector named Clyde who, quote, "doesn't trust paperwork that only exists in email."

She was scribbling a note to herself in the lobby when a deep voice called out behind her.

"Excuse me, Miss. Are you Jabari Henderson?" A deep voice said.

She turned, startled.

A tall, dark-skinned, older black man in a well-worn suit approached, grinning widely beneath a short salt-and-pepper mustache. His badge read *J. Spencer: Public Services.*

"Yes, sir, I am," she said, cautiously as he shook her hand.

"Thought so. I'm Jasper Spencer, JCSU class of '89. I heard we had a Golden Bull making waves up in here," He said with a big grin.

Her face lit up. "You're an alum?"

"Proud one. And even prouder of you. Congratulations on winning that grant, young lady."

Something loosened in Jabari's chest.

Mr. Spencer wasn't flashy. He was calm. Solid. Like somebody's favorite uncle who gave good advice and always had a bottle of cold ginger ale in the fridge.

"Crown and Glory is doing something important," he said. "That daycare's gonna help folks. It's a strong project with a broad foundation: churches, colleges, city, and state. That's how you build resilience." He winked, "I know because I help write the community grants."

Jabari nodded, "Thank you, sir. That means a lot."

He gave her his card. "Come to me if you hit a wall. Been around for a while. I don't do everything, but I know how to get things done."

She tucked the card into her folder as if it were gold.

By the time she left the building, Jabari was exhausted but energized. The tiredness that comes after winning a small battle in a much bigger war.

The permits weren't provided. The inspections weren't done.

But now, she had *names.* She had *numbers.* She had allies.

And most importantly, she had proof: this system didn't move on its own, people pushed it. Through relationships. Through showing up in person, looking someone in the eye, and saying, "I care."

This IRL stuff has its benefits, she thought, smiling to herself.

For the first time in weeks, she didn't feel like she was falling behind.

She felt like she was catching up, learning the rules, earning her space, and rewriting what it meant to lead.

Check-In

Jabari

Jabari rolled up to Crown and Glory's side entrance with a tote bag full of permit folders and a head full of what-ifs.

She had more names now. More numbers. However, no inspections have been scheduled, and no official approval has been stamped. She wasn't panicking. Not exactly. But anxiety hummed in her chest like bad wiring.

Abike buzzed her in.

"Come on back," she called from the breakroom.

When Jabari entered, she found the new mother at the small table near the microwave, nursing baby Malik with a calmness that made Jabari immediately self-conscious about her own twitchy energy.

"Sit," Abike smiled. "You look like you haven't blinked since Tuesday."

Jabari laughed weakly and dropped into the seat across from her. "City Hall went well," she said, opening her folder. "I met a few people who actually care and a few who made it clear I should avoid them like raw chicken. Still waiting on the fire and electrical inspections," Jabari said, flipping through her folder, "and, uh… I have a major problem."

Abike looked up, eyebrows raised.

"I stopped by the electrician's business address today," Jabari continued, her voice tight with frustration. "The place was cleared out. Empty. Sign gone. The mail is piling up on the floor under the mail slot. Looks like he skipped town."

Abike didn't flinch. In fact, she *laughed*, warm and low like someone who'd been there, done that, and built a business anyway.

"Jabari, I cannot tell you how many contractors I went through before Crown and Glory opened. Half of 'em ghosted. One guy kept promising me permits he never even applied for. Another tried to bill me for 'spiritual cleansing' of the space."

Jabari blinked. "You're joking."

Abike grinned. "I wish."

Jabari nodded. "Yeah. He left the wiring half done, and I can't plug anything in until we pass the electrical inspection."

Abike nodded, adjusting the blanket draped over Malik. "Let's think about a backup plan. Tell me the worst-case scenario."

Jabari hesitated. "The permits don't come through in time."

"And?"

"We can't open our doors to the children."

Abike didn't flinch. "Okay. Then we delay."

Jabari blinked. "But—"

"You're doing the necessary work. You're following up. You're making connections. *It will be fine.* But if it isn't fine immediately? We pivot."

She rocked Malik gently as she spoke. "You've told every parent that the opening date is *tentative.* Nobody expects miracles. They want a quality daycare from the moment the doors open. Even if we need to push things back a week or two, we'll still throw the open house party. Still meet the parents. Still train the staff."

Jabari frowned, slowly exhaling. "I just don't want to disappoint you."

Abike smiled. "You're not disappointing anyone. You're building something real and you're building it *right.* This ain't a race. And a delay doesn't change the *value* of what you're doing."

Jabari closed her folder. "I just... I thought if I didn't hit every mark, it meant I failed."

"Baby girl," Abike said gently, "success is not precision. It's persistence."

Malik gave a small sigh, milk-drunk and happy. Abike kissed his forehead and held him close.

Jabari watched the whole moment, the intimacy, the ease, the *home* that lived in that woman's arms. Then Dana walked in from the back entrance, grease on her hands and softness in her eyes.

“Hey,” she said. “Y’all good?”

“We’re good,” Abike said.

Dana leaned over, kissed Malik’s head, then gave Abike a quick kiss on the mouth. Nothing dramatic. Just love, casual and firm, like it had always been there. Dana thoroughly washed the car grease and grim from her hands and lifted her son from Abike’s arms.

“I’ll start looking for an electrician tomorrow.” Jabari grimaced.

From the corner, Dana perked up while gently burping a very sleepy Malik over her shoulder.

“Electrician?” Dana asked. “Is that why wires are still hanging out of the walls, babe?”

“Yeah, the electrical contractor skipped town. After we open the daycare, we can pursue him legally for our deposit and breach of contract. Don’t have time for that now.”

Dana grinned. “Let me check around. I know a couple of instructors at Central Piedmont, the community college. They work with students coming out of the electrical trades program, and they usually know which local businesses do *good* work. Reliable, licensed, not flaky.”

She adjusted Malik, who let out a tiny, sleepy sigh.

"I'll text you some names tonight. Might even get a discount if they get their hair done here," she added with a wink.

Abike smiled at her wife with love and adoration. "Salon sister perks."

Jabari felt something in her chest shift.

Not envy. Not quite.

Yearning.

She didn't have that with Lamont. She never had. Not the tenderness. Not the alignment. Not the ease. They were always offbeat, reaching past each other in different rhythms.

Dana and Abike were in sync. And it looked beautiful.

And suddenly, it didn't seem so strange that she'd been thinking about Celeste's laugh or her lip gloss or the way her voice dipped low when she got serious.

That kind of connection… could be mine too. It just happened to be between two women.

Later, as Jabari walked back out to her car, her shoulders felt lighter. The checklist still existed, but it no longer ruled her.

She was building something. Not just a daycare. Not just a career.

A *life*.

A whole, rich, community-rooted, love-possible kind of life.

And now… she knew what it might look like.

CHAPTER 6

Dinner at Jabari's Apartment

That evening, Celeste knocked on Jabari's apartment door with a bottle of $7 wine and sore feet. Jabari opened the door barefoot in a Black-owned-brand T-shirt and leggings. Her smile was soft and a little tired.

"Tonight's dinner is brought to you by Chef UberEATS," Jabari said.

"And the wine is fancy, as in, I didn't buy it from a gas station," Celeste added, handing Jabari the bottle.

Jabari reached for the food and handed Celeste a container of Thai curry noodles. Celeste curled up on the couch in sweatpants and a tank, her hair freshly twisted, her skin glowing from what looked like a proper post-salon steam and scrub.

They ate out of takeout boxes on Jabari's couch like they'd done it a dozen times. The wine flowed easy, the laughter even easier.

"Why is car ownership a full-time job? I'm from Brooklyn, my people didn't own cars!" Celeste groaned. "Like, I didn't ask for all this stress."

"Uh oh, sounds like you got Dana's responsible car care lecture." Jabari laughed.

"Yeah, a bit intimidating. I'll need a car journal to keep up with all the things I'm supposed to keep an eye on. But I can't complain. Dana got my car purring like a kitten. She even cleaned it, so it looks brand new. You betta believe I paid attention.

"Someone should have told me this stuff a long time ago. It would have saved me money and heartache. Dana was like a caring big sister. She wanted to ensure I had reliable transportation in case I needed to get out of a sticky situation quickly."

"Oh yeah, the 'if he acts a fool, bump him with the tires and drive to safety' speech!" Jabari giggled, "I got that lecture, too."

They both laughed. "This 'adulting stuff' is no joke. I don't know how my mom did it with us kids. How did she feed us? Between school loans, car insurance, groceries, health insurance, and professional licensure fees, it feels like every time I turn around, I've got to pay someone."

"And what is that '*FICA deduction*' on my check?" Jabari added, "I didn't *consent* to this."

Celeste howled with laughter, nearly choking on her noodles.

They laughed until their faces hurt, the space between them closing with every joke, every shared sigh.

"You *did it*," Celeste said, grinning. "You kicked the bureaucracy's ass."

Jabari flopped beside her, letting her head fall back against the cushion. “I wouldn’t say I *kicked* it… more like I wrestled it into a tired mutual respect.”

Celeste laughed. “Same thing.”

They clinked glasses with a soft *chime*, and the evening unfolded around them like warm fabric, slow and unrushed.

After dinner, barefoot and loose from the wine, Jabari leaned into the couch’s armrest, watching Celeste sip and smile.

“I met Abike and Dana’s baby today,” Jabari said. “He’s this soft little cloud named Malik, and Abike’s just… so chill with him. Like she was born with that calm.”

Celeste raised a brow. “And Dana?”

“Total grease-under-her-nails vibe, but she holds that baby like he’s made of gold. They’re like… I don’t know, a *power couple*. But soft. Not performative. Authentic.”

Celeste nodded. “Yeah. They’re the blueprint.”

Jabari paused. “I’ve never been around that before. Two women, that kind of love, a kid, a *life* together. It wasn’t just romantic, it was *anchored*.”

Celeste’s face shifted, thoughtful, then hesitant.

“I’ve dated women,” she said softly. “Always have. But it never looked like that. Not like what they have.”

She took another sip, then set the glass down.

"I don't call myself a 'lesbian'," she continued, making air quotes with her fingertips. "Not because I'm not into women. I am. Always have been. But that word? It's never felt like *me*."

Jabari tilted her head. "Why not?"

Celeste shrugged slowly. "It just... feels heavy like it belongs to white women in documentaries and rainbow flag rallies. Not girls from Flatbush who kissed their best friend behind the bodega."

Jabari didn't laugh. She just *listened.*

"I've always felt love, desire, and sex outside of language. It wasn't a rebellion. It just *was.* The label never fit because the love was layered. Nuanced. Political by default but not by declaration. And when Black women love each other?" Celeste's voice softened. "There's a whole unspoken language under the surface, a different rhythm. The world doesn't have words for that. You have to experience it."

Jabari was quiet for a long time.

"Damn," she said finally. "You're deep."

Celeste smiled. "The wine helps."

They both laughed, but the quiet returned, not awkward, just reflective.

Jabari turned her head and met Celeste's gaze, open, warm, a little vulnerable. Not pushing, not pulling. Just *there.*

"I'm glad you're here," Jabari said. "I didn't know I needed this. But I did."

Celeste nodded. "Me too."

A beat passed. Then, slowly, Jabari leaned forward and pressed a soft kiss to Celeste's forehead.

Celeste closed her eyes for a second, letting it land.

When she opened them, Jabari had already leaned back, not rushing, just steady. Celeste gave her a quiet smile.

"Thanks for dinner," she said softly.

"Anytime," Jabari replied, her voice just above a whisper.

And in the space between them, something settled.

Not romance. Not yet.

Texts with Friends

Jabari

Jabari stood in her kitchen, staring into the fridge like the answers might be in the orange juice.

She wasn't a teenager. This wasn't her first crush. But this felt *different*. Bigger. Quieter. Scarier.

That forehead kiss had been instinct. Soft, safe, and loaded.

Her thumb hovered over her phone screen. She opened a chat with her college line sister, Tierra, who'd been there through every bad relationship and midnight panic session in college.

Jabari: *Okay, don't freak out. But I wanted to kiss a girl last night.*

Tierra's reply was instant.
Tierra: *Okay, WHO?! And did you or nah??*

Jabari: *I didn't. But I wanted to. Her name's Celeste. She works at the salon. And like… being around her just feels* **GOOD.** *Like, not perform-for-you good. Just… real. I'm bugging right??*

Tierra: *Girl, no. You're FEELING. That's what's new. And look, feelings don't gotta come with labels right away. But if you wanted to kiss her? That means something even if you're still figuring it out.*

Jabari exhaled. She wasn't ready to say more. But Tierra's words stayed with her.

This wasn't about suddenly becoming something new. It was about recognizing something true.

Celeste

Celeste lay on her bed, scrolling through Instagram with one hand and her group chat with the other.

Her friend Yvonne had already noticed the shift.

Yvonne: *You quiet today. Who got your curls soft like that??*
Celeste snorted. She typed.

Celeste: *This girl, Jabari. She works next door. She hugged me yesterday. Kissed my forehead last night: no moves or pressure. There was something about it that made me feel held, like really* held. *It scared me a little.*

Yvonne: *You ever felt that before*?

Celeste paused.

She'd dated girls before. Hookups. Flings. One ex in hair school who was sweet but emotionally closed off. It had always been sexy, sometimes fun, but never... safe and never seen.
Celeste: *Not like this. It wasn't even sexy like that. It was just...* right. *Like my body was like, "Yes. Stay here." And that's scarier than any label, to be real.*

Yvonne: *Real ones hit different. You don't gotta know what it is yet. Just don't run from it.*

Celeste locked her phone and stared at the ceiling. Yani was right. Jabari hadn't made a move. But the energy between them buzzed like a live wire.

It wasn't about whether Jabari was "gay enough" or wore a label like a name tag.

It was about how Jabari made her feel: respected, calm, and curious. A little unsteady. But not in a bad way.

Like she was starting to trust something.

Intentions

Celeste

Celeste lay in bed, one arm tucked behind her head, staring at the ceiling like it might offer answers. The city moved outside her window , cars passing, cicadas singing, someone's bass heavy in the distance. But inside, it was calm.

She kept replaying that soft kiss on her forehead. Jabari's voice was low and sincere. The way they just *sat together* with wine and takeout, as if it wasn't complicated.

It was the most grown-ass thing she'd done in months.

She thought about the other couples she'd been around lately: Abike and Dana, steady and solid, with that baby boy running their whole world. Bevanne and Kia, parenting a whole crew of boys and somehow still flirting like newlyweds. And Dawn, who moved like someone who had a story but wasn't about to tell it unless the roof was on fire.

Don't ask Dawn about her personal life, Celeste thought with a smile. *If she wants you to know, she'll drop it in your lap.*

But one thing was clear: those women had depth in their relationships. Not just heat. *Home.*

Celeste's past?

She thought about her past relationships, if she could even call them that. They were mostly sex and vibes. Some with women who didn't even claim it. Some who disappeared when things got real. Some who were fire but burnt out quick. Most didn't want to build anything, and she hadn't demanded more.

Back then, she didn't think she needed more.

She didn't regret any of it. Sex had been a language she spoke fluently. She'd explored, learned, and indulged. But lately... she wanted something *else*. She needed emotional safety. She needed to be known.

Celeste laughed to herself.

Bonding, not just boning. Who am I, Maya Angelou? Still, it hit deep. She wanted that now. Or at least... she was *open* to it.

She thought about Jabari's earnest soft, brown eyes and nervous laugh. The way she looked so proud, sharing her victories from City Hall.

And maybe, just maybe, this friendship with Jabari would grow into that kind of closeness.

Maybe, Celeste thought, *we could build something real.*

But only with time. Only if it was mutual. And only if they stayed honest. She'd never rush it, though. Jabari was still figuring things out, and Celeste respected that.

She'd wait. If it bloomed, it bloomed.

And if not?

She'd still found a *real* friend.

But for now, something about the possibilities with Jabari made her want to sharpen up in life, at work, and in how she showed up.

Time to step it up

Celeste

The next day, the salon was steady, back-to-back appointments, blow dryers, loc care, and laughter bouncing off the mirrors. Celeste worked with renewed focus. Her parts were cleaner. Her curls tighter. She moved with intention.

During the afternoon lull, she caught sight of Abike handing baby Malik off to Solomon, who held him like he was cradling royalty.

"Be gentle," Abike said, adjusting the strap on the baby carrier. "That baby runs my whole life now."

"Doesn't even have teeth," Solomon said, grinning. "Already your boss."

"You're not wrong."

Celeste waited until Abike returned from her daycare walk-through with Jabari before knocking lightly on the office door.

"You got a second?" she asked, peeking into the chaos of pacifiers and baby wipes.

Abike glanced up from behind her desk, where Malik's blanket had taken over the keyboard. "Sure. Come in. Mind your step. If you can find floor space."

Celeste stepped in carefully, avoiding a rogue teething ring. "You weren't kidding about him running things."

Abike laughed. "Who knew someone who can't talk, tell time, walk, or read would be managing my schedule, home, and business? Part of the reason I applied for the daycare grant was to have decent childcare nearby."

"You love it," Celeste teased.

Abike's face softened. "Yeah, I do."

She nodded toward the chair. "What's on your mind?"

Celeste sat. "I just wanted to check in. Say thank you. And maybe ask for a little advice."

Abike leaned in. "Shoot."

"I've been thinking about how to grow, not just survive the chair, but *build something* here. A real career. A brand. Something that lasts. I'm skilled with my hands, but I want to take it further. I just don't know how."

Abike nodded slowly. "That's a real growth mindset. Most folks don't even know *how* to ask that question."

She paused, then started ticking off fingers. "Okay. First? Start thinking about entering local stylist competitions. Build your portfolio. Not just selfies but real editorial-style shots. I've got a camera somewhere in this office. Ask around for clients willing to model."

Celeste leaned forward, "You think I'm ready for that?"

"I think you're hungry for it. That's enough to start."

Abike kept going. "We get asked about stylists for photoshoots, weddings, stage events. Most of us turn them down. It takes too much time, and we all have too many family obligations. But you? You've got flexibility. If you've got makeup skills, you'd be unstoppable in that space."

Celeste nodded. "I've done some gig work; brows, eyes, light contour. Nothing major."

"That's already more than half the girls out here claiming MUA in their bios. Get your kit ready. You could be a one-stop shop for wedding parties. Just know, those clients can be *intense*. But they pay."

Celeste chuckled. "Noted."

Abike leaned back, brushing a braid off her forehead. "And if you're serious about long-term growth, think about taking business classes. CPCC. Central Piedmont Community College has courses for entrepreneurs. I think some are free."

Celeste hesitated. "I'll check. Might have to wait, though. I'm still recovering from my last rent check."

Abike gave her a knowing look. "If CPCC doesn't cover it and you find the right class, come back to me. We may be able to help with the cost. Especially if it's tied to building up Crown and Glory."

Celeste blinked. "You'd do that for me?"

Abike smiled. "You're part of the team. We invest in each other. That's what makes this different."

Celeste left that office *buzzing*. Her chest is full and her mind racing, not with worry this time, but with vision.
She could do this.

She didn't need to be perfect. She didn't need all the answers. She just needed a path. And now? She had one.

Work. Grow. Build.

And maybe... *love.*

But that part could wait. For now, she had a mirror to stand behind, a camera to find, and a future to shape.

Later That Night

Jabari

The city settled into itself.

Streetlights blinked on. AC units hummed low. Somewhere, wind chimes knocked against a porch railing in the dark.

Miles apart, Celeste and Jabari lay in their separate rooms, both curled toward the soft light of their nightstands. Their phones close.

Jabari, heart still tapping an uneven rhythm, stared at the ceiling. She hadn't *kissed,* kissed Celeste. A quick kiss on the forehead was nothing serious.

But she'd wanted to.

Not out of heat or impulse, but because something *inside* her felt pulled, anchored, curious. Like her spirit was already a few steps ahead, waiting for her to catch up.

She rolled onto her side and reached for her phone.

Deep breath.

Jabari: *Hey… random idea.*
There's a Food Truck Friday at Freedom Park this week. You wanna go with me?

She hovered over the screen for a beat, thumb uncertain.

Then she hit send.

Celeste

Celeste saw the screen light up.

Jabari's name.

Her heart jumped, a *little* more than it should've.

She read the message once. Then again. A slow smile crept across her face.

No pressure. Just a vibe. Just *them*.

She typed:

Celeste: *That sounds perfect.*

And just like that, something moved forward.

Not declarations. Not labels.

No name for it yet, but they were both willing to find out.

Together.

CHAPTER 7

Food Truck Friday

Jabari

The air smelled like jerk chicken, buttered elote, and something deep-fried and unapologetic. Freedom Park was alive.

Families strolled past booths. Aunties posted up at picnic tables with strawberry lemonades and folding fans. Kids zigzagged around tables with ice cream-sticky fingers. A live band on the small stage played go-go covers of Beyoncé hits, and nobody complained.

Jabari walked past the mango sorbet stand, scanning the crowd for Celeste. She spotted her by the barbecue truck, waving with a foam tray in one hand, curls catching the evening light just right.

"There you are," Jabari said, smiling wide.

Celeste raised an eyebrow. "You're late."

"I'm fashionably present."

"You lucky I saved you the last jerk salmon taco."

They found an open patch of grass near a cluster of picnic tables. Both sat cross-legged on a blanket. They ate in happy silence for a few minutes, trading bites and fighting over who got the last plantain.

"This one lady," Celeste said, mouth half-full, "she tried to book me for an 'express silk press and style' at 6:45 yesterday. We close at seven."

Jabari choked on a piece of rice. "What'd you say?"

"I blinked at her until she backed away."

They cracked up together. The music swelled in the background, the horn section kicking in just as the sun dipped below the trees.

They watched the crowd move, the dancers up front twirling with joyful chaos, the toddlers bobbing in rhythm with no sense of timing. Jabari leaned back, exhaling.

"This is exactly what I needed," she sighed.

Celeste leaned back, too. "Right? Just good food, good weather, and not a single spreadsheet in sight."

Jabari smiled, but her eyes were scanning the field. "Is that... Bevanne?"

Celeste followed her gaze. Bevanne was in gym shorts and a "Hair Raised Me" tee, tossing a baseball underhanded to a little boy who caught it with both hands and squealed. Kia stood nearby with their other son, offering loud encouragement. Other children and adults were playing as well. Bevanne's family. They were a tribe unto themselves.

Celeste waved, and Bevanne spotted her immediately. She waved back, "Did you see Dawn? She's cooking in the New Bethel food truck, selling fried fish for her church group." Bevanne then pointed at Jabari with mock sternness and called out, "Permits ain't gonna pull themselves!"

Jabari shouted back, "Working on it!"

Kia gave them a thumbs up. One of the boys waved with both hands. Celeste felt something sweet and heavy tug at her chest.

"This community," she said, almost to herself. "It's real."

Jabari nodded. "Yeah. And I didn't realize how much I needed it until I was neck-deep in it."

A little girl ran by with her hair in puffballs and glitter across her cheeks. Her dad jogged behind her, holding a cup of lemonade and two paper plates.

Jabari leaned forward slightly, watching them. "I keep thinking about what it'll feel like when Children of the Dream finally opens. You know? Like, not just the paperwork, but the actual noise. The children. The energy. I want that."

"You'll get it," Celeste said softly. "You're already building it."

Jabari turned toward her then, golden brown eyes warm and full. Celeste was so cute. ...no beautiful. "You always say the right thing," she said.

Celeste smiled, brushing lint from her thigh. "Nope. I just see what's in front of me."

The band kicked into a groove that made people jump to their feet. Jabari tapped her foot along with the beat. Celeste bobbed her head.

"Dance with me?" Celeste asked, suddenly bold.

Jabari blinked, surprised, but not by the question. By how quickly her body answered for her.

"Yeah," she said. "Yeah, okay."

They left the blanket, walking into the crowd, slipping between kids and aunties and hype dancers until they found a spot and just let themselves move.

It wasn't a club scene. It was more sweaty than sexy. But it was pure joy.

Pure. Unfiltered. Moving in rhythm with a girl who made your chest feel too small for your heart.

And for the first time in a long time, neither of them felt like they had to try.

Sweet Things

Celeste

They danced until the band took a break, breathless from laughter and two-stepping around toddlers.

Jabari's curls were frizzing at the edges, and Celeste had her shoes in her hand, holding them like a prize as they made their way back through the crowd.

"Okay," Celeste panted, "that counts as cardio. I don't want to hear anybody say I don't exercise."

Jabari was laughing too hard to answer at first. "Girl, my thighs are screaming."

They stopped by Dawn's food truck. The church food truck had run out of fish and were packing up for the evening. Dawn was seated at a picnic table close beside a quiet woman. "This is my girl, Sara. Sara, honey, these are the new girls I been talkin' 'bout, Celeste and Jabari."

"Nice to meet y'all." Sara said, "Good work on the Dream grant, Jabari. Please let me know if you need any It technical support. I'm a professor at JCSU. We worked hard on that grant, and we are so proud of y'all."

Jabari ducked her head, uncomfortable with so many people knowing about her project. "Thank you, Ma'am. I'll certainly keep you in mind."

Dawn winked at them, "We saw y'all dancing. Look good out there."

Jabari and Celeste continued past the dessert trucks lined along the edge of the park. The smells were almost rude; warm cinnamon, powdered sugar, real vanilla, and fried dough.

Celeste grabbed Jabari's arm. "Wait. I smell funnel cake."

"Oh no," Jabari groaned. "You're not gonna drag me into powdered sugar hell."

"You owe me," Celeste said, mock-serious. "You said you'd get dessert."

"When?"

"Doesn't matter. I heard it. It's canon now."

Jabari sighed dramatically. "Fine. But if I end up sticky, you're holding the napkins."

They stood in line behind a trio of teenagers debating whether to opt for Nutella drizzle or the classic. Jabari leaned in close, not quite touching, but warm. Present. Celeste felt it, every inch of that near-touch.

They split a funnel cake under a pop-up string of lights, finding a quiet spot on the hill just past the stage where families had started packing up. Above them, the sky was a soft navy, with stars blinking through the light pollution as if they were trying to get noticed. The moon was low and fat and golden.

Celeste licked sugar from her thumb. "This right here," she said. "This is my idea of luxury."

"Sticky fingers and mosquitoes?" Jabari asked, smiling with those pretty brown eyes.

"Yup. People I love, good music, and dessert I didn't have to make. That's wealth."

Jabari nodded slowly. "You're not wrong."

They sat in silence for a moment, watching a family walk past with sleepy kids on their parents' shoulders.

Celeste shifted, her knee brushing Jabari's. This time, she didn't pull away.

"You ever feel like," Celeste said, voice low, "you're waiting for your life to start? Like you're in it, technically, but not all the way inside yet?"

Jabari didn't answer right away. She just nodded. "Sometimes I feel like I'm doing everything *right*, checklists, plans, degrees, but I still don't feel like an adult. Just... busy."

Celeste leaned back on her hands. "Same. Like, I'm *doing* things. But when I finally get a minute to breathe, I'm like... is this it? Is this the whole deal?"

Jabari looked over at her then. Her profile was soft in the dark. Her lashes curled just so. Her lips still held a trace of sugar.

She wanted to kiss Jabari. So badly it made her chest tight.

Jabari turned, sensing it. Their eyes locked, and the air shifted.

A breath. A heartbeat.

Jabari didn't move. Celeste didn't either.

But the tension buzzed between them; tender, heavy, patient.

Instead of kissing, Celeste reached over, plucked a bit of powdered sugar from Jabari's cheek, and let her fingers linger just a beat too long.

"Thanks," Jabari whispered. Her voice sounded like something she didn't mean to say out loud.

They looked away at the same time. Not embarrassed. Just... overwhelmed by the intimacy of not acting. Jabari chuckled to herself.

"What?"

"Nothing," she said. "Just... learning how to sit in it."
Celeste didn't press. She just nodded and leaned her shoulder against Jabari's.

They finished the funnel cake in companionable silence, the music fading, the crowd thinning. But neither of them made a move to leave.

Ghost Signal

Jabari

Jabari's phone buzzed.

She ignored it.

They were still sitting shoulder to shoulder on the hill, the last bits of powdered sugar clinging to the paper tray between them. Celeste was telling a story about a middle-schooler's DIY relaxer gone wrong, and Jabari was laughing, genuinely, until the phone buzzed again. And again.

She pulled it out of her pocket with a sigh.

Lamont (3 texts): *Hey, can we talk? I miss you.*

Jabari's stomach dropped. The sweet in her mouth turned metallic. Guilt pressed behind her eyes like a migraine just getting started.

Celeste paused mid-sentence. "Everything okay?"

Jabari swallowed. "It's my ex. Lamont."

"Oh," Celeste said, neutral.

"He's been... I mean, we've been doing the long-distance thing since graduation. But it's not really working. We're kind of in this weird—" She trailed off, realizing how it sounded. "It's complicated."

Celeste blinked, then looked away. "Got it."

Jabari hated the silence that followed. She felt like she'd cracked something between them; something warm and growing, and now it was spilling through her fingers.

"I didn't mean not to tell you," Jabari said, voice low. "I just… I forgot about him, honestly. That's messed up, right?"

Celeste nodded slowly, still not looking at her. "A little."

It wasn't said with malice…just truth.

"I mean, I didn't *do* anything," Jabari added, suddenly defensive, unsure who she was trying to convince.

"I didn't say you did."

Jabari exhaled, heart racing for all the wrong reasons now. "I just… I don't know what's wrong with me. One minute I'm thinking about kissing you, the next I'm reminded I have this whole relationship hanging in limbo."

Celeste's jaw tightened. "Sounds like you gotta figure that out."

There was no heat in her voice. That's what stung the most. She wasn't mad. She was just… stepping back.

And Jabari could feel the space growing between them with every heartbeat.

"Maybe I should get going," Celeste said, standing and brushing off her legs. "Got an early shift tomorrow."

Jabari wanted to stop her. To explain. To say *I didn't mean for this to get messy.*

But all she managed was a quiet, "Yeah. Okay."

"Thanks for the night," Celeste said, voice even.

"Celeste—"

"You don't owe me an explanation," she said, quick. "We're not… anything. It's fine."

That hurt more than it should have.

"But I want to explain," Jabari said, her voice threading between apology and plea. "It's complicated."

Celeste nodded slowly, not looking at her. "It usually is."

There was a long pause.

"Goodnight, Jabari."

Celeste didn't ask for a ride. Didn't wait to be walked out. She gave a short wave and disappeared into the crowd like smoke.

Jabari sat on the hill alone, her phone still buzzing in her hand, her heart louder than the band warming up again in the distance.

Whatever she was building with Celeste had just hit its first crack.

And she didn't know if it would hold.

CHAPTER 8

Cracks in the Frame

Celeste

"Y'all ever have a night where you think the vibe is *vibing* and then boom; she got a boyfriend?"

Celeste said it half-joking as she tied an apron around her waist the next morning, but the hurt was sitting just behind her eyes, pulsing.

Bevanne looked up from her station, one eyebrow raised. "Wait, *what*?"

"Jabari. Miss Early Childhood Development. Turns out she's got a man-long-distance, but still."

Dawn wheeled her stool over, holding a coffee like it was holy. "Oh, *she's* the one you were giggling about on Tuesday. I knew something was brewing."

Celeste shrugged, tugging her curls into a high puff. "Yeah, well. Apparently, it's a triangle. And I didn't even know I was a side."

"That's rough," Bevanne said gently. "But... did she say she was in a full relationship?"

"She said it was complicated," Celeste muttered. "But she also said she forgot about him, which is... I don't know. That's mess, right?"

"Could be honesty," Dawn said. "Could be confusion. Could be both."

"I just hate feeling like I misread it." Celeste's voice cracked a little. "Like I thought we were building something soft. Something safe. And I walked right into a wall."

Bevanne reached out, warm hand on her arm. "Sometimes people carry old love too long. Doesn't mean what they feel for you ain't real. But it does mean they've got work to do."

Celeste nodded, but her chest still hurt.

She'd let herself hope. And hope, when it hits the ground, always lands hard.

Jabari

What the hell was she doing?

She'd spent weeks building something real; with the daycare, with herself. And maybe, maybe, with Celeste. But she still hadn't shut the door on a relationship that had been limping for years. Now, the weight of that indecision had just cost her something she wasn't even ready to admit she wanted.

Lamont was calling again.

Jabari stared at his name, lighting up her phone screen from where it sat on the kitchen table next to her untouched breakfast.

She didn't answer.

She couldn't.

Instead, she called Tierra.

"You sound stressed," Tierra said, no greeting needed.

"I messed up. With Celeste."

"You mean forehead-kiss girl?"

Jabari groaned. "Yes. I didn't tell her about Lamont until after we had this *moment.* And when I did, I could feel her shut down."

"Do *you* even still want Lamont?" Tierra asked plainly.

Jabari rubbed her temple. "I don't know. We've been together since our sophomore year. He's... familiar. Comfortable."

"Comfortable and connected ain't the same thing," Tierra said. "You didn't forget him because you're a monster. You forgot him because *she* made you feel present."

Jabari blinked. That hit a little too close.

"She's different," she admitted. "It's like... with Celeste, I don't have to shrink or explain myself. I can just be."

"Well," Tierra said, "then the question isn't about Celeste. It's about you. Are you ready to stop living in the relationship that you've already outgrown?" Tierra was an expert at getting to the heart of the matter.

Jabari wanted to grow, not stop at familiar, comfortable, or convenient.

Jabari didn't answer right away. But the silence *was* the answer.

Later – Crown and Glory

Celeste

Celeste was washing a client at the bowl when she saw Jabari standing outside through the front window. Waiting.

Bevanne looked at her with a slight tilt of the head. "You want me to get her to leave?"

Celeste shook her head. "No. Let me finish this rinse. I'll go talk to her."

The water ran warm and steady, but Celeste's chest was tight with nerves. This wasn't over. Not yet.

But she wasn't sure if she wanted closure or clarity.

Or maybe, somehow, both.

Real Talk

Jabari

Celeste met Jabari outside the salon, arms folded, eyes steady. “You wanted to talk?”

Jabari nodded. “Yeah. If you’ve got a minute.”

Celeste motioned toward the side alley; quieter than the main strip, shaded and private. They walked in silence, the air thick with something too heavy for small talk.

They sat on the low brick ledge behind the salon. Celeste didn’t look at her right away. “I’m not mad,” she said finally. “But I was hurt.”

Jabari took a breath and nodded once. “You had every right to be.”

“I just...” Celeste paused. “That moment with you; it felt like something. And I thought I could trust what I was feeling. But then hearing about your boyfriend after... it made me feel like I was reaching for something that was never really mine.”

“You weren’t,” Jabari said quickly. “You weren’t reaching alone.”

Celeste looked over, eyebrows lifted. Waiting.

“I messed up,” Jabari admitted. “I should’ve told you about

Lamont before we got that close. And not because I was trying to play you. I just... being with you felt like a break from all of it. From expectations, from figuring myself out, from doing what's always felt safe."

Celeste softened just a little, but her voice stayed firm. "So where does that leave him?"

"I don't know," Jabari said honestly. "We've been dragging it out, long-distance, out of habit more than love. But last night? Sitting with you under those lights, wanting to kiss you? That felt more real than anything I've had with him in months."

Celeste looked away, teeth tugging at her bottom lip. "I need to know I'm not someone's experiment."

"You're not," Jabari said. "I don't have all the answers yet. About labels. About where I fall on the map."

They were quiet again. A car rolled by on the next street over. Inside the salon, someone laughed loud enough for the sound to reach them. Life kept going, even here in this stillness.

Celeste turned back to her. "I'm not asking you to figure it all out overnight. But I can't hold the weight of two relationships; one you're in and one you're thinking about."

Jabari nodded, tears stinging. "I don't want to do that to you."

Celeste looked at her, finally. "So what do you want?"

Jabari inhaled. Slow. Steady. "I want to be honest. With you.

With myself. I want to end things with Lamont the right way and not carry that guilt into something new. But I also… I don't want to lose whatever this is between us while I do that."

Jabari went on with more determination, "I know what I feel when I'm with you. And it's not confusion. I want to spend time with you, see you smile, laugh together, talk with you about my hopes and fears, and hold each other when we cry. And heaven help me, I desire you so much, I have to restrain myself from kissing you head to toe every time I see you." Jabari shivered at the last bit. This was raw honesty.

Celeste exhaled slowly and smiled. "Then we need space, just a little. Until you're clear, I'll be here, but not halfway. Okay?"

"Okay," Jabari said. "That's more than fair."

They stood slowly, still facing each other. The tension was still there, but so was the respect. And maybe something more substantial underneath it.

"I meant what I said last night," Celeste added, voice softer now. "Being around you *feels* different. But I need it to feel whole. Not tangled."

Jabari smiled through the ache. "I want that too."

They hugged briefly, and not like before, not charged, not yearning. Just two people learning how to move through a real thing with care.

As they pulled apart, Jabari said, "Thanks for not shutting the door."

Celeste gave her a small, real smile. "Just don't make me regret it."

No Going Back

Jabari

Lamont picked the restaurant, a sports bar with greasy wings and three muted TVs showing different games. Jabari sat across from him, sipping water, waiting for him to actually *see* her.

He didn't.

"You got your little daycare job," he said, mid-wing. "But that doesn't mean you're too busy for your man."

Jabari blinked. "Lamont… I'm managing a build-out, writing reports, and wrangling city inspections. This isn't just a job. This is *my career*."

He scoffed. "It's not that deep. You make sure babies don't eat crayons."

Jabari sat back. Stunned. "Wow."

"What?" he said, like she was overreacting. "You're acting like you're running a hospital."

"I'm running something that matters," she said, calm but clear. "And I need people in my life who respect that."

Lamont leaned back. "You saying I don't? So wait, you found somebody else?"

She closed her eyes. "This isn't about anyone else. It's about me choosing peace. Choosing myself. For once."

His silence turned sour.

"Wow," he muttered. "You think you're better than me now. Got your grant money and your soft-ass job and think you're too good for the man who held you down." Lamont's jaw tightened. "You are changing, Jabari. Ever since you got that grant. And since you started hanging with that salon crew."

"Stop," Jabari said, voice low.

He paused, surprised.

"You're not going to turn this into jealousy or shame," she said. "I've carried this relationship long enough. And I'm done feeling guilty for growing. I need someone who has my back. Not someone who wants to keep me small. I'm not better," she said quietly. "I'm just done."

Lamont blinked, mouth half-open.

Jabari stood.

"This is over," she said, simple and free. "And I'm okay with that."

She left before he could argue. She didn't look back.

And she didn't cry. Not this time.

The Promise

Jabari

That night, Jabari lit a candle on her desk and sat in the glow. No music. No phone. Just stillness.

She thought about Celeste, the softness in her voice, the strength in her silence.

She wanted to earn that smile again.

And this time, she wouldn't offer half of herself.

She'd be honest. About Lamont. About where she'd been. About where she wanted to go.

And if Celeste still wanted to meet her there?

She'd build something real.

Slow. True. Rooted.

She whispered the words aloud, just to feel them in her mouth:

"I want this. I'm ready."

CHAPTER 9

In Her Element

Celeste

Inside Crown and Glory, Celeste was focused. Confident. Her hands moved with purpose, rhythm in every braid, loc, and twist.

Bevanne watched from the doorway, nodding with pride. "You know your sections look cleaner lately?"

Celeste grinned. "I've been practicing on my mannequin head at night."

"You might be ready for the back-to-school hair rush," Dawn added, slipping her a fresh edge brush. "Those mamas gonna be asking for you by name."

Later that day, she did a full cut and style on a new client, a struggling mom who hadn't had her hair done in months. Celeste took her time, listened to the woman's story about her hard times, and when she turned the chair for the final reveal, the woman teared up.

"You made me look like myself again," she whispered.

Celeste smiled. "You never stopped. I just brought it forward."

Applause came from Bevanne, who had watched the whole thing from the shampoo bowl. "Okay, miss thing. That's a Crown and Glory moment."

That Afternoon Outside the Salon

Celeste

Celeste had just swept the last of the hair into the bin when she saw Jabari standing outside the salon, back near the alley where they first met.

She wiped her hands, nodded at Bevanne, and stepped out.

Jabari looked up, unsure. "Hey."

Celeste nodded once. "You said you wanted to talk?"

Jabari gestured toward the side alley, where it was quiet, shaded, and familiar.

They stood in the same spot where they had first found each other, tears in their eyes, only this time they were upright. Steady. Barely.

Jabari

"I ended it with Lamont," Jabari said, skipping the preamble. "I did it in person. And I made it clear; no open doors. No maybes. We're done."

Celeste folded her arms. "Why?"

"Because I couldn't keep dragging that past into something that could actually become *real.*" She exhaled. "And because you deserve someone who shows up for you fully. Not halfway. Lamont and I have been over for a long time. It was long past time I ended it for good."

Celeste's eyes softened. "That's... good to hear."

"I should have told you about Lamont. I should've ended it with him sooner," Jabari admitted. "But I didn't want to lose what we were building. So, I took the coward's way and waited. That wasn't fair to you, and I'm deeply sorry."

Celeste leaned against the wall. "Thank you for saying that."

They stood there a moment.

"I know I hurt you," Jabari said. "But I want to work to rebuild that trust. I want to *earn* you, not just charm you."

Celeste smiled faintly. "That's a good line."

"It's not a line," Jabari said, stepping closer. "It's a promise. I'm not perfect. But I'm learning, growing. And I want you to be part of that, if you still want me."

Celeste took a long breath. Her voice, when it came, was low but clear.

"I've been in flings. Fast ones. Messy ones. But I've never had someone come back to me with *this*. With clarity, honesty, and intention." She moved closer too, just enough that Jabari could feel the heat between them.

"This," Celeste said, "this is adult woman energy. And I respect that."

Jabari looked at her, lips parted, eyes wide, still a little afraid to hope.

Then Celeste leaned up and kissed her.

Soft. Sure. A kiss that said: *I see you. I* feel *you. I'm still here.*

Jabari's breath caught, her clit throbbed, and her knees nearly buckled.

When they broke apart, Celeste nuzzled her neck and whispered, "Now get out of here before I make you late for your next inspection."

Jabari blinked, dazed. "Damn, my *toes curled*, Celeste! What did you do to me?"

Celeste walked backward, grinning as she opened the salon door. "Just keeping my promises."

The door closed behind her.

Jabari stood there, stunned, her heart thudding in her chest like a drumline.

She kissed me like she meant it, Jabari thought. *Like we have a real chance.*

And for the first time, that thought didn't scare her.

It thrilled her.

CHAPTER 10

First Date

Celeste

The sky over Charlotte was a rich blue-purple when Celeste pulled up to Jabari's apartment in her newly tuned-up Sentra. Dana had worked her magic. The engine purred. No sputtering. No dashboard warning lights. And it was not only cleaned, but detailed. For once, her car wasn't arguing with her about existing.

Celeste stepped out in wide-leg, dark denim that hugged her hips just right, and a bone-colored crop top that showcased her toned arms and a sliver of midriff. Her gold anklet glinted above a pair of clean sneakers. Her skin glowed a deep bronze under the soft streetlight, her curls defined and shaped into a high puff, sleek and sharp.

She felt like a grown-ass woman. Centered, nervous, but ready.

Before she could even knock, the apartment door opened, and there stood Jabari.

Tall and honey-brown, her figure wrapped in a cream sleeveless jersey dress that hugged every damn curve from shoulder to calf. The neckline dipped just enough to hint at softness without giving away the whole plot. Her natural hair was sculpted into a halo of coils, part of it pinned back with golden cuffs. Her hoops caught the light, and her scent, lavender and something warmer, drifted forward as she stepped aside.

"You look..." Jabari trailed off, taking her in slowly, deliberately. "...edible."

Celeste laughed, low and satisfied. "I'll accept that."

"You wore that on *purpose,*" Jabari said, grinning.

"Guilty. You too."

"I almost put on sneakers," Jabari said. "But I wanted you to see these hips do what they do."

"Oh, trust," Celeste said, glancing over her shoulder as she stepped in, "they're doing it."

They didn't rush to leave.

They stood in the middle of Jabari's living room, orbiting each other like gravity had a plan. Not touching, not yet, but close. There was no tension, no noise. Just chemistry. That rich, full-bodied kind you could breathe in like incense.

Dinner was at a tucked-away Black-owned spot in the NoDa arts district; warm lighting, lush plants, and tables made for leaning in close. The playlist ran from Solange to Ari to Cleo Sol without missing a beat. Every drink was named after a literary icon.

Celeste wore her confidence like fragrance. Jabari was a whole mood.

The waiter couldn't stop glancing at Celeste, visibly fumbling when she smiled. But Celeste didn't even notice. She was focused on Jabari; completely, unapologetically.

Jabari noticed. And liked it.

"You really don't see that man drooling every time you blink?" she asked after he left.

Celeste blinked. "Who?"

"Exactly."

They ordered cocktails. Celeste got the "Zora Neale Mule" with a splash of passion fruit, and Jabari got the "Morrison Jazz" with hibiscus and ginger.

"I'm glad we're doing this for real," Celeste said, tracing the edge of her glass.

"Me too. Like, fully present. No secrets."

Celeste's tone shifted slightly; honest, steady. "I should say up front… I've always dated women. Since high school."

Jabari raised an eyebrow, curious. "Yeah?"

"I knew I liked women, always have. But the term 'lesbian' never quite fit. Too stiff. Too white-woman-on-NPR. The *word* never felt like it was made with someone like me in mind. Love between Black women? That's something else. More layered. More fluid. Half the time it ain't even about sex. It's about feeling... *seen.* I don't need a label for that."

Jabari swallowed, eyes soft. "You make it sound like poetry."

Celeste chuckled. "It's deep love. But yeah, sometimes poetry too."

"I've always dated men," Jabari continued. "Not because I was trying to hide anything. That's just who showed up. Until you."

Celeste's lips curled slightly. "So, I showed up and ruined the algorithm?"

Jabari laughed. "You showed up and... reset something. I don't know how to explain it."

"You don't have to," Celeste said. "You just have to be real."

Jabari took a breath. "You're my first. Woman, I mean. First, I've wanted like this. Not just in theory. Not a girl crush. Not just any woman. I want *you.*"

"I don't know if I'm into *women*, plural," Jabari said. "But I am into *you.* Like, all the way."

Celeste didn't react immediately. She gave Jabari time to own her words.

"I'm not confused." Jabari added earnestly, "I'm not experimenting. I just... didn't expect to feel this kind of clarity with someone who wasn't what I thought I wanted. But now? I want you... desire you. You're all I can see."

Celeste reached across the table, hand palm-up.

Jabari took it without hesitation.

"You don't need to explain it," Celeste said, thumb stroking gently. "I feel it. And that's enough."

They ate slowly, trading bites, stories, and laughter. Letting intimacy fill the small space between them like warm light. These weren't butterflies. This was gravity.

This was *pull.*

Jabari

Later, on Jabari's balcony, the air was velvet soft. They sat under a thrifted blanket, sipping two glasses of wine and gazing up at a sky full of scattered stars.

The kiss didn't rush.

It waited.

It leaned on the hush between stories and found a quiet beat where time paused.

Celeste cupped Jabari's face, gentle, steady. "Still sure?"
Jabari nodded. "Surer than anything."

Their mouths met; soft, slow, *intentional.* Jabari's whole body responded like she'd been tuned for this very moment. Celeste tasted like red wine, and certainly.

There were no fireworks. It was firewood: Slow-burning, heat-building, room-filling desire.

And it was *earned.*

When they finally pulled apart, Jabari exhaled like she hadn't realized she was holding air.

Celeste caressed her back. "So… still breathing?"

"Barely," Jabari said, dazed. "I think I forgot how lungs work."

Celeste laughed low and ran a hand down Jabari's arm, "Don't pass out now. That was just a preview."

Jabari swallowed. "Yes, I'll try to remember to breathe." She sounded pretty breathless.

Celeste just laughed, full and free, already knowing she'd be the one driving Jabari wild with that kind of power, not through pressure, but through patience.

That Night

Jabari

The balcony kiss had burned gently, but now the burn deepened into heat.

Celeste looked at her...like *really* looked at her, eyes sweeping over Jabari's skin like she was already memorizing it.

"You sure?" Celeste asked, voice low, body still.

Jabari cuddled closer, her heart thudding like it was trying to speak for her. "Yeah," she said softly, feeling Celeste's warmth surround her. "I want this."

Celeste's touch was featherlight under her jaw. "Then let's talk for a second."

Jabari nodded, her pulse high in her throat.

Celeste kept her eyes steady and her voice calm and sure. "No games. No pain. No performance. I'm not into being penetrated-not tonight, not most nights, but I love touching, tasting, giving. That cool with you?"

"Yes," Jabari said, without hesitation. "Completely. And... I should say, I've never had sex without a condom. I got tested after Lamont and I broke up. I'm negative across the board."

Celeste nodded. "Same. I get tested regularly. And thank you for telling me. That matters."

Jabari exhaled. "This is all new to me. I've never... with a woman, I mean."

Celeste's expression softened. "That's fine, baby. You don't have to know anything except how you feel. I'll take care of the rest. Just say what feels good. Or if it doesn't."

Jabari's voice caught a little. "Okay."

"Good," Celeste whispered, leaning in close with a soft kiss. "Then let me in."

They stepped inside, the quiet hum of Charlotte's night rising behind them as the sliding door shut. Jabari's fingers slipped down from Celeste's hand, then back up to her waist, unsure but wanting.

"You good?" Celeste asked.

"Yeah," Jabari whispered. "Just nervous."

Celeste leaned in, pressing her forehead to Jabari's. "Nervous means you care. Let me take care of you."

Jabari nodded.

They kissed in the hallway, deeper than before, slower. Jabari's back pressed to the wall, and Celeste's hands framed her hips like art. She dragged her fingertips under the hem of Jabari's wrap dress, nails grazing warm skin.

Jabari let out a shaky breath. "God..."

Celeste smiled against her lips. "Nah. Just me tonight, sweet thing."

In the bedroom, their laughter melted into silence. Jabari let Celeste pull the dress from her shoulders. The fabric dropped slowly, puddling around her bare feet. Jabari wore a black lace bra with matching panties. The cotton crotch of the panties was soaked. Jabari had been excited all night, and the wetness between her thighs was a testament to that fact.

Celeste stepped back.

"Damn," she said, her voice reverent. "You are something else."

Jabari flushed. Her curves, her softness; the hips, the way her breasts rose and fell with every breath, they all felt suddenly sacred under Celeste's gaze.

"Girl," Celeste said, stepping in close, "you are so beautiful, Jabari. We fit in ways I never thought."

Celeste kissed Jabari, deep and slow, before she took her time undressing. The crop top came off first, then her jeans. The bra and underwear were next. No hesitation. Celeste was comfortable in her own body, not shy at all. Her skin was smooth caramel, her body firm, toned, and powerful. Her breasts were tipped with milk chocolate areolae and erect nipples. Jabari watched, mouth parted.

"You're..." Jabari tried to say something, anything, but she just gaped like a goldfish. *I'm drooling!* Celeste was gorgeous.

Celeste grinned. "Yeah, I know. So are you, babe."

Celeste's caresses made Jabari shiver. Jabari's bra was removed, and her heavy breasts were free. Celeste's warm touches over her back, arms, and waist were intoxicating. Jabari managed to touch Celeste, too, but too lightly, causing Celeste to giggle.

They laughed, breathless, as they tumbled onto the bed. Jabari lay under Celeste, wrapping her arms around her waist, and her thighs cradling her firm body. Celest was right, they fit well together. Celeste's curves and weight were just the right amount of pressure. Jabari melted into full body contact with Celeste, caressing her curves in wonder.

Celeste kissed her again, this time while trailing fingers over Jabari's breast. She paused, looked up.

"This okay?"

"Yes," Jabari whispered, her eyes fluttering shut as Celeste's mouth closed around her nipple.

She gasped.

Her back arched as heat surged through her. "Damn… Celeste…"

"I love how your body talks to me," Celeste murmured, switching sides, licking and sucking until Jabari whimpered under her touch. "You are so responsive. You are beautiful, babe."

Celeste kissed her way down, across Jabari's waist, to her belly button, and over the soft skin of her inner thigh. Jabari was trembling as hands massaged her hips and sides. Jabari sighed and gasped at sensitive spots, giggling at ticklish ones. Celeste thoroughly mapped each area. Jabari followed her every move, wide-eyed, hands moving over Celeste's warm skin in awe.

Celeste paused at her thighs. She raised Jabari's thighs and spread them wide, opening her wet labia to reveal the glistening, darker lips within and an erect, hooded clit. Celeste kissed the inside of her thigh and inhaled the scent of her sex. "Tell me what you need."

Jabari looked down, her brown eyes wide, pupils dilated. "Everything, Just... don't stop."

"Any part of this off-limits?"

"No," Jabari said, panting, voice trembling but certain. "Nothing. ... be careful."

Celeste smiled at Jabari's loss for words as her body began to speak up. "Always."

Then she dipped her head and licked a slow, deliberate caress between her wet slit and over Jabari's clit.

Jabari cried out, her hands flying to the sheets, her hips lifting off the bed. " Oh-oh, Celeste!"

Celeste hummed in response, circling her tongue and then sucking gently, steadily, never rushing. She read every twitch, every sigh, every sharp intake of breath.

Jabari felt her slide one finger inside, slow and smooth, curling perfectly.

Jabari moaned deep from her chest. "Holy fuck! Yes..." Jabari's hips lifted into her, her moans higher now, desperate.

"Too much?" Celeste asked, pausing her tongue just long enough.

"Don't stop!"

Celeste added a second finger, curling just right, licking just right, until Jabari unraveled with a full-body shudder, crying out her name like a prayer. "Ahh, Celeste!"

Celeste added a second finger, adjusting the rhythm; her mouth and hand working in sync.

And Jabari *shattered.*

She came hard, louder than she expected, her body clenching, thighs trembling, voice cracking as her breath came in broken gasps.

She collapsed back, panting, stunned.

But Celeste wasn't done.

She moved up beside Jabari, kissing her breasts again, soft and gentle this time, massaging her stomach. Jabari trembled with each touch.

Celeste slipped her wet fingers back between Jabari's thighs, barely touching, just brushing her now-hypersensitive skin. Jabari gasped again, more startled than anything.

Jabari blinked. "Wait... I thought we were done."

Celeste smiled. "Baby, we just got started."

Then Celeste flicked her clit. *Lightly*.

That was all it took.

Jabari jerked, sobbed once, *just once*, and came again.

She covered her mouth with both hands, stunned. "Jesus...what —"

Celeste just held her through it, stroking her side as she trembled and cried out, her body rocked by aftershocks.

The third time came without warning.

Celeste whispered in her ear, "You're so beautiful, Jabari. I love how you smell, how you taste, how you come all over me. You are perfect." And nipped at her shoulder, then slid two fingers inside, finding a slow, deep rhythm, no rush. Jabari was limp, helpless, but still moaning as the tension built again and spilled over in one last wave when Celeste hit that sweet spot inside.

She spasmed hard, back arched, lips parted, and eyes closed. "Celeste!" She said in wonder, "I've never...like this..."

Done.

Spent.

Undone.

“You okay?” Celeste whispered, breath warm against her ear.

Jabari nodded against her. “Yeah, that was... that was...How did you??” She couldn’t finish. Jabari lay on her back, chest rising and falling, skin glistening with sweat.

Celeste curled beside her, kissing her shoulder, brushing her hair back gently. When Jabari shivered with cold, Celeste pulled the comforter over them and pulled her close.

“That was...” Jabari, hoarse, tried to speak. “That was everything.”

Celeste smiled, slow and warm. “You did good.” Reaching beside the bed, Celeste handed her a bottle of water.
Jabari drank deeply, realizing how dry her throat was. “Oh, God. Was I loud?”

“No worries, the neighbors only banged on the wall once.” Celeste grinned.

Horrified, Jabari said, “Please tell me you’re joking.”
“I’m joking.”

“Thank God! I would never be able to look my neighbor in the eye again.”

Jabari held Celeste lightly and kissed her thoroughly. Jabari turned toward her, eyes still wild but soft. "Can I... touch you now?"

Celeste shook her head gently. "Not tonight. I'm good."

Jabari looked momentarily unsure.
Celeste kissed her forehead. "Doesn't mean I don't want you. Just means tonight was for you. All you had to do was feel."

Jabari bit her lip, eyes locked on Celeste. "I've never had anyone do that. Not just... make me feel that good. But make me feel safe, comfortable, free..."

Celeste pulled her close. "Then get used to it." They lay tangled in each other, the air thick with sweat and the scent of sex. Celeste kissed her and then curled behind her, spooning Jabari close, arms wrapped around her middle like armor. Celeste chuckled, holding her tighter. "Sleep, babe."

Jabari let herself go, not just slipping into sleep, but into *trust*.

Celeste stayed awake a few minutes longer, watching the rise and fall of Jabari's chest, her hand resting protectively over her belly.

She smiled.

They had time.

This was the beginning.

CHAPTER 11

Morning Light

Jabari

The sunlight was soft through the blinds, cutting faint gold lines across Jabari's bedsheets. She stirred before Celeste, their bodies still tangled; one of Celeste's legs thrown lazily over her thigh, a hand resting on Jabari's stomach like it had always belonged there.

Jabari lay still, eyes open, watching the dust float through the light. Her chest rose slowly. Full. Lighter than it had felt in months.

It had been real; all of it.

The talking. The touching. The intensity. The care.

And now, the after. Stillness. Warmth.

She glanced down at Celeste, whose curls spilled onto her shoulder. Peaceful, even in sleep. One hand curled slightly against Jabari's skin, like her body knew not to let go.

Jabari swallowed.

This felt big. Bigger than anything she'd called "love" before. And yet, it wasn't overwhelming, not the way love had felt with Lamont. That had been loud, demanding, and heavy.

This?

This felt like a door opening.

Celeste shifted slightly, then blinked awake, squinting at the sun.

"Hey," she murmured, voice husky and low.

"Hey," Jabari whispered back, brushing a curl off her cheek. "Sleep okay?"

Celeste nodded. "You?"

"Best I've had in... years."

Celeste smiled slowly, then kissed her shoulder. "We grown for real now."

Jabari laughed, quiet but deep. "So... what are we?"

Celeste looked up, her expression open but unreadable. "You tell me."

Jabari inhaled. "I want to be with you. Not just sleep with you. Not just text and flirt. I want... the day-to-day. The showing up. I want to learn how to do this right."

Celeste's eyes softened. "Then we'll take our time. But we're a *we*. Okay?"

Jabari smiled so wide it almost hurt. "Okay."

They lay in silence a little longer, soaking in the comfort of clarity. No games. No confusion. Just two Black women figuring it out, soft and honest.

After breakfast that morning, Jabari stretched like a cat, feeling deliciously sore from the previous night's sex. She cuddled next to Celeste with her coffee. Still high on endorphins, she said, "How did you do that to me so easily?"

"Do what?" Celeste sounded mighty smug.

"You know," Jabari blushed, ducking her head.

"Use your words, Jabari." Celestes laughed, "Too late to be shy."

Jabari took a deep breath. "Ok, full disclosure. No one has ever brought me to orgasm that easily before. And they were powerful orgasms. How??"

"I've had some practice." Celeste sounded serious. "But it's mainly you, babe. Your body is a delight. You're so sensitive and responsive. Your body tells me what to do. You're easy to please. It also helps that you are polyorgasmic."

I'm what? Jabari asked in confusion.

"Polyorgasmic. You can come multiple times with little to no refractory time between orgasms. Didn't you know?" Celeste said, genuinely concerned. "How has it been in the past?"

Jabari, a little embarrassed, said, "Half the time I faked orgasms. Lamont always rubbed my clit too hard or pounded into me until I was sore. He seemed pleased. Usually, I was just ready for it to be done. I was lucky to have an orgasm. After he came, he immediately went to sleep. And he was the best of my past boyfriends....at least he knew about the clitoris. I've never had three orgasms in a row like last night. It felt wonderful."

Celeste looked at Jabari for a long moment. "Huh. How rude. Granted, I've never had sex with guys, but that sounds terrible." Cuddling Jabari close, she said, "Babe, you have been done a grave disservice. I promise to be a better lover. I'll show you things and teach you about this wonderful body of yours. There will be no need to fake it. And please tell me if anything is the least bit uncomfortable. Sex is a conversation, a poem, a song. It has rhythm, rhyme, and a melody."

Jabari had thought she was just a poor lover and that having orgasms were, really, hard. But there was little conversation before, during, or after sex, and especially with Lamont. Celeste was constantly checking in with her during sex to make sure she was ok. There was also a steady stream of compliments, praises, and encouragements last night that kept them connected. Maybe her prior relationships were bad, which led to barely bearable sex. Regardless, she had a lot to learn.

"Thank you, Celeste. I had no idea," she said quietly. "I can't wait to use what I learn to blow your mind like you have blown mine."

Celeste laughed long and hard. "Once you get the hang of all this, I have a feeling you will be insatiable, my dear. And I can't wait."

Jabari joined in the laughter because Celeste was not wrong. She could already feel the delicious desire for Celeste's kisses. She was definitely hungry for more. They cuddled together, spending a lazy Saturday on the couch watching movies.

CHAPTER 12

Sunday Call Home

Jabari

"Jabari, baby, you sound tired. Are you sleeping enough?"

Her mother's voice came through the phone warm and concerned, with that baked-in Virginia softness that Jabari could never quite match, no matter how many years she'd lived in Virginia.

"I'm fine, Mama. Just a long week."

"Well, I hope you're still eating real food and not all that college junk."

"I'm not in college anymore, remember?"

"You know what I mean." A pause. "How's the center coming?"

Jabari rubbed her temples. "Messy. Better. I met some city folks who are gonna help me push things through. I've got inspections next month, and a waitlist already."

"Oh, so folks are lining up? Look at God."

Jabari smiled, but it didn't reach all the way. There was still so much she couldn't say.

Her mom meant well. But she'd always kept things tight, square, predictable. *Childcare Center manager* was a job title her mom could understand. The growing feelings Jabari had toward Celeste? That was a different kind of territory.

"I'm proud of you," her mom added. "You always were a good girl."

Jabari swallowed. "Thanks, Mama."

They hung up with a long "love you" and a "call me next Sunday," and Jabari sat still for a moment. Her apartment was quiet except for the hum of the fridge. The silence left space for that new question to rise again:

What happens if who I am doesn't fit who they expect me to be?

Sunday Dinner Drama

Celeste

Celeste was elbow-deep in dishwater when her mom shouted from the living room: "You know they're hiring down at the bank, right? Full benefits. You could get off your feet!"

Celeste clenched her jaw. "I *like* doing hair, Ma."

"I'm just saying. It's not a forever job."

Celeste scrubbed harder. Her mom had been on this kick for years. She didn't consider styling to be real work. Just something cute until Celeste got serious. Never mind that clients were already asking for her by name.

Her younger brother, Asa, wandered into the kitchen, snagged a juice, and hugged her. "You know how she is. You want me to distract her while you sneak out?"

Celeste grinned at him, "Appreciate you."

Back at her apartment, Celeste texted Bevanne for the name of that stylist retreat she'd mentioned once, a weekend workshop in Asheville with natural hair educators and business training. She was serious about this career and determined to build her skill set, even if no one in her family understood her vision. Maybe Jabari would enjoy a weekend in Asheville after the center opens.

Her phone buzzed again.

A new text from Jabari.

Jabari: *Still thinking about Friday night. Wow, just wow!*

Celeste smiled, warmth blooming low in her chest.

Jabari: *I desire more. Just so you know, I'm addicted.*

Celeste: *Lol. Most definitely, I got you.*

Jabari: *Hope your Sunday's been smooth.*

Celeste: *It's had its bumps. But I'm good. You?*

Jabari: *Same. Family is family. But I'm learning not to fold.*

Celeste: *That part. Talk soon?*

Jabari: *Always.*

Celeste tucked her phone under her pillow and stared at the ceiling.

In the Light

Celeste

Later that week, Celeste stepped into Crown and Glory with a little more curve in her walk, a little more hum in her throat. Her hair was in a slick puff, edges laid, and her gloss was fresh.

Dawn clocked it before Celeste even hit her station.

"Alright now," she called, sipping her hibiscus tea. "You got a *glow* this morning."

Celeste grinned, twisting her apron on. "Must be the new bonnet I slept in."

"Uh-huh. And who you sleepin' *with* in that bonnet?" Bevanne teased from the reception desk.

Celeste waved her off, but the blush creeping up her cheeks betrayed her.

The salon doors jingled.

Jabari stepped in with a stack of flyers for the daycare open house, wearing jeans and a cropped tee, her locs up in a bun, with subtle lip gloss that was absolutely showing out.

Celeste's whole face softened without even trying.

Jabari walked over, cool but warm. "Hey."

"Hey," Celeste said, voice low.

They didn't touch, not here, but the current between them was unmistakable. Dawn raised an eyebrow. Kia, who'd stopped by to drop off snacks for the break room, shot Bevanne a knowing look.

Jabari handed Celeste a flyer. "Open house next weekend. We'd love y'all to come through."

Celeste looked at her — really looked — and nodded. "I'll be there. We'll all be there."

As Jabari turned to leave, her fingers brushed Celeste's just slightly, just long enough for Celeste to close her eyes for half a second and let the electricity settle.

When Jabari was gone, the room fell into a moment of exaggerated silence.

Then Dawn broke it.

"So y'all together or y'all just sharing flyers and pheromones?"

Celeste grinned, not even pretending anymore. “We’re figuring it out.”

Bevanne leaned over and whispered, “That girl makes you look *happy.* Keep hold of that.”

Celeste did.

CHAPTER 13

Almost There

Jabari

The daycare was buzzing. The walls were being painted in bright, earthy tones — affirmations stenciled over doorway arches in pastel vinyl letters:

"You are worthy."
"You are your Ancestors' Dream."
"Grow with love."

Jabari moved between rooms with a clipboard; her phone balanced on her shoulder as she spoke to a city liaison.

"I've submitted the last sanitation compliance doc, and we've got the foam mats installed. You're saying we're still missing something?"

She paused, listened, her expression darkening.

"Well, nobody told me about the emergency exit signage needing to be *bilingual and in Braille.* That wasn't on the daycare checklist."

Another pause. Jabari exhaled hard. "Okay. It's the city building code. Okay. I'll figure it out."

She hung up and leaned against the wall of the toddler room, heart thudding—stupid regulations. *A blind person would not have time to search for the Braille sign in an emergency anyway. We would lead them out.*

They were supposed to be days from opening. Parents were already confirming attendance. The stylists were hyping it up to their clients. Everything was riding on this.

Her phone buzzed again; this time from Celeste.

Celeste: *Hey, I was thinking I'd bring you lunch in a bit. Sandwich? Smoothie?*

Jabari stared at the screen, guilt creeping in. She didn't feel like smiling right now. But she also didn't want to push Celeste away.

She typed fast:

Jabari: *Actually, maybe not today. Kinda drowning over here, city being city. Catch you later?*

Celeste saw the dots. Then nothing.

Misread

Celeste

She stared at her phone longer than she meant to.

It wasn't the message itself. It was the *pullback*. The "*catch you later*" that felt like a brush-off.

She knew Jabari was under pressure. But they'd agreed to *show up*, even when things got hard.

Celeste exhaled, setting the phone down on the break room table. Dawn peeked in just then, eyes squinting.

“You alright?”

Celeste nodded too fast. “Yeah.”

“You sure? You look like someone just skipped a hug after promising one.”

Celeste gave a half-smile. “We’re just… adjusting. You know. It's been just a week since we became a thing, and now she’s buried in city mess. I get it.”

Dawn stepped closer. “It’s okay to be understanding. But don’t let ‘understanding’ mean ‘quietly hurt.’”

Celeste nodded again, slower this time. “Yeah. You right.”

Making It Right

Jabari

Hours later, Jabari walked into the salon holding two smoothies and a bag of warm, foil-wrapped sandwiches.

Celeste looked up from her station, surprised. Her client had just left. The timing was suspiciously perfect.

“I shouldn’t have brushed you off earlier,” Jabari said, walking closer. “I let stress talk for me.”

Celeste took the smoothie, cool against her palm. "I wasn't mad. Just... felt it."

"I want us to be a team," Jabari said. "Not something I treat like a luxury I only reach for when things are easy."

Celeste's eyes softened. "That's a grown sentence."

Jabari leaned in, lowering her voice. "You're the only soft thing I have in my life right now. I don't want to handle you with rough hands."

Celeste touched her arm. "Then don't. But let me hold some of the load too."

Jabari nodded, relief showing in her whole body. "I'm gonna need you next week. Big time. We're still not cleared for inspection."

"Let's get it done," Celeste said. "And then celebrate properly."

They didn't kiss, not here, but the way they looked at each other, they might as well have.

CHAPTER 14

Stress, Soaked Away

Jabari

Jabari sat on the floor of Celeste's apartment, staring at her to-do list like it was a death sentence.

"I swear I'm gonna have an ulcer," she whispered.

Celeste walked in, arms behind her back. "Then we're shutting this evening down."

"What?"

"No more lists. No more email. Get up."

Celeste pulled her gently to her feet and led her to the bathroom. The tub was already filling. Lit candles. Soft music. A bottle of **Dawn's Famous Herbal Spa Bubble Bath**, its label half-worn from love.

"Dawn said this one's lavender, calendula, and something called 'Holy Patience.'"

Jabari snorted. "Gotta love the Salon Sisterhood."

Celeste helped her undress slowly, reverently. Once she was in the tub, Celeste slipped in behind her. She massaged her shoulders from behind, fingers kneading with just enough pressure to settle her soul.

"You're not doing this alone," Celeste whispered.

"I know," Jabari said, tears pricking her eyes. "I just... want it to be perfect."

"It already is. Because it's *yours.*"

Let Me Try

Jabari

After the bubble bath, Celeste and Jabari lay in bed. Relaxed, just quiet.

Just *them.*

Jabari rolled onto her side and looked at Celeste, eyes soft.
"I want to touch you this time."

Celeste raised an eyebrow. "Oh yeah?"

"I mean... for real. Not just hands wandering. I want to *learn* you. Like, learn what makes you feel good. Let me try, if you're open to that."

Celeste smiled, slow and wide, voice low and teasing. "You're trying to make me fall deeper, huh?"

Jabari grinned. “Already happened.”

Celeste leaned in for a kiss, warm and slow, before pulling back just enough to whisper: “Then take your time. I’m all yours.”

They traded kisses and smiles. Celeste lay back against the pillows, legs parted, one arm behind her head. Nipples dark and erect on honey-colored breasts. She was soft and powerful, curves glowing in the low light, eyes full of patience and promise.

Jabari straddled her, suddenly shy again. “Tell me what to do.”

Celeste reached up, brushing her fingertips along Jabari’s jaw. “Start by listening.”

“To you?”

Celeste shook her head gently. “To *me*. My body. My breath. How I get goosebumps when I get close. The way I shift when something feels right. Let your hands ask questions. Feel my body answer.”

Jabari nodded. Taking Celeste in, Jabari said, “You are gorgeous, Celeste. I’m so privileged to be with you.”

She kissed Celeste’s neck, chest, and stomach, stopping to suck gently at the soft skin of her breast, licking the nipples. When she gently blew a cool breath over the wet nipples, they puckered tight and erect.

Celeste moaned. "Oh, babe, that tingles."

Jabari's hands gently massaged her waist and hips, feeling the faint twitch of muscle underneath. She inhaled the scent of bubble bath, the spicy Thai noodles they had for dinner, and the unique scent of Celeste's arousal.

Celeste exhaled. "That's good. Softer now... yes."

Jabari kissed and suckled each nipple before she moved lower, her hands running along Celeste's thighs, hesitant but hungry. Desire pushing her.

"You don't have to rush," Celeste murmured. "There's no finish line. Just *explore*."

Laughing, Jabari moaned, "I'm trying to go slow, but I just want to touch you all over!"

How about this, babe?" Celeste adjusted her position, so her thighs scissored between Jabari's thighs. Jabari sighed as she ground against her thigh, getting the friction she needed.

They kissed deeply and groaned into each other as they rutted against the firm pressure of their thighs. Celeste shivered as she left a wet trail on Jabari's thigh. The friction sensation was delicious against her clit.

Jabari's wet labia left soft kisses along Celeste's thigh as they undulated together, moaning and panting with stimulation. The kisses became more frantic as they moved.

Jabari shifted again. Pulling Celeste's thighs up and out, revealing her moist labia and generous clit. Carefully, she descended over Celeste, letting their wet labia and clit kiss. She could feel Celeste's erect clit nudge against her clit. "Celeste, this feels so good! I've never..." Each touch sent shivers down her spine. She watched as Celeste's skin began to break out in goosebumps.

Celeste shuddered, "Oh, babe! That feels so good. Don't stop." Celeste stiffened, stopped breathing, and let out a loud panting moan. Her pupils were blown, and she spasmed uncontrollably with each clit kiss. Jabari leaned down and kissed her thoroughly with a smug grin.

"You good, Celeste?"

Celeste took a moment to catch her breath, "Fuck yeah, babe! Always knew you'd be a quick learner."

"I have an expert teacher who gives private lessons," She giggled.

Adjusting her position again, Jabari dipped her head between Celeste's legs, breath warm against her. She kissed her labia, tentative at first, then pressed her tongue forward, slow and focused on the juicy pink clit nestled in the dark flower of labial folds.

Celeste let out a soft moan. "Right there... just like that. Little circles...oh, oh, babe!"

Jabari adjusted, watching for every breath, every shift, every hum of approval. She licked again, slower this time, savoring the taste and feel of making Celeste *unravel.*

She applied pressure with her palm over the hot wet lips. Celeste arched, her hands gripping the sheets. "Yes, babe. That's it. You're doing so good!"

That praise hit Jabari deeper than she expected. She moved with more confidence, tongue working rhythmically, mouth never leaving the heat of her clit.

Celeste's moans deepened; no longer coaching, just *feeling.* Her body rocked into Jabari's mouth, her thighs trembling.

"Don't stop," she whispered. "I'm right there—"

Jabari didn't. She held on, stayed with her, followed every twitch and gasp until Celeste came hard, calling her name through gritted teeth. "Ahh, Jabari!"

Afterward, Celeste pulled her up and kissed her deeply, gripping her face in both hands.

"You've *absolutely* been paying attention."

Jabari grinned, flushed and glowing. "You're a very patient teacher."

Celeste pulled her close, panting, their foreheads touching.

"You didn't just make me come," she said softly. "You made me feel *loved.*"

"Celeste, you *are* loved," Jabari said solemnly.

"Oh, babe, so are you." Celeste sighed into another deep kiss. "So are you."

They lay there together, legs tangled, hearts beating in sync.

It wasn't about mastering technique.

It was about showing up. Fully. Freely. Fearlessly.

And that? *That* was making love.

CHAPTER 15

A Baby and a Dream

Celeste

Two days before the opening, Abike arrived at the daycare with Malik in a sling and a giant pack of construction paper butterflies for the window display.

Celeste was already there. She held Malik on her hip while Jabari and Abike adjusted signage on the front door.
"He likes you," Abike said.

Celeste bounced him gently. "He knows I've got snacks."

Malik gurgled in agreement.

Jabari stepped back and looked at the almost-ready space: furniture set, paint dry, toys organized. Bright colors. Soft light. Hope in every corner.

She took a breath. "It's really happening."

Celeste came up beside her, baby still in arms. "You made it happen."

Jabari looked at her, really looked, and smiled.

"No," she said. "*We* did."

The Inspection

Jabari

Jabari paced the front room of the daycare, clipboard clutched like a life vest. Her button-down shirt was ironed. Her smile, not so much.

Elaine, the electrician, was running checks on the last outlet. Abike sat in the office, feeding Malik and keeping one eye on the clock.

Celeste arrived with coffee.

"Survival brew," she said, handing Jabari hers. "Vanilla oat milk. No ulcer ingredients."

Jabari took it with shaking hands. "What if I missed something?"

"You didn't."
"What if I *think* I didn't, but I actually did?"

"You didn't."

Before she could spiral further, the door opened and in walked a woman in city-issued navy and sensible flats, carrying a tablet.

"Ms. Henderson?"

Jabari stepped forward. "Yes."

"I'm here for your final daycare inspection."

Abike whispered, "Go time."

Twenty-Two Minutes Later

The inspector stood at the doorway with her tablet, stylus poised.

"Emergency signage; verified. Infant room ventilation; verified. Fire hydrants, as designated. Electrical panel new installation; passed. Playground surface; meets state safety grade."

Jabari held her breath.

The inspector looked up, face unreadable.
"You're clear to open."

Jabari blinked. "I'm...what?"

"You passed. Congratulations."

Celeste whooped so loud she startled Malik, who burst into happy shrieks in Abike's arms.

Jabari just stood there, stunned. Then slowly, she smiled. Big. Bright. Unrestrained.

Celeste wrapped her in a tight hug, lifting her off the floor.

"You did it," she whispered.

"No," Jabari whispered back. "We *did it.*"

Grand Opening

The sidewalk outside Children of the Dream was covered in chalk drawings and balloons. A hand-painted banner read:

NOW OPEN!

**CHILDREN OF THE DREAM DAYCARE:
SAFE. NURTURING. OURS.**

Inside, the rooms bustled with parents touring, kids testing toys, and stylists dropping off little ones before appointments.

Bevanne showed up with Kia and their boys in matching dashikis. Dawn handed out mini containers of her herbal lotion with the new daycare logo printed on the lid.

Even Dana came by, muttering, "Y'all better not ruin my wiring."

The mayor's office sent someone to snap pictures as they cut the ribbon. And yes, Mr. Spencer had *indeed* expedited that permit. He was there politicking, shaking hands, and kissing babies.

Jabari walked the floor like a woman reborn; confident, relaxed, still stunned by her own power.

Celeste stood near the door, greeting families, her hand occasionally brushing Jabari's as they passed.

One mom leaned over and whispered, "Y'all are *too* cute. That daycare-love vibe."

Celeste winked. "We keep it professional. Mostly."

Later That Evening

The crowd thinned. Solomon was cleaning up. The music faded. Malik slept in a carrier. Celeste handed Jabari a sparkling cider in a solo cup.

"To you," she said. "To this place. And to the love that built it."

Celeste raised her cup. "To Black women making magic out of thin air."

They toasted, then held each other for a long, quiet moment, surrounded by the space they had built, not just the daycare, but the relationship, the confidence, the *life*.

"You ready for what comes next?" Celeste asked.

Jabari nodded. "Yeah. I think I finally am."

EPILOGUE

Bright Future

That fall, the mountains called.

Celeste's Sentra hummed along the winding curves of the Blue Ridge Parkway, fresh from Dana's tune-up, the engine smooth as butter. Jabari rode shotgun, curls wrapped in a silk scarf, and a camera in her lap, snapping photos of the blazing reds and golds outside the window. They stopped often, on overlooks and side pull-offs, posing, laughing, holding hands in selfies with the sweep of Appalachia behind them.

Asheville was both a getaway and a milestone. Celeste had entered the city's renowned Natural Beauty Expo; her first real competition since joining Crown and Glory. And she didn't just show up, she placed. **Second place for makeup. First place for natural loc color and style.**

Jabari had screamed so loudly when her name was announced that she was hoarse by dinner.

They spent the long weekend at the Grove Park Inn, curled up in oversized rocking chairs in front of the massive stone fireplace each night, mugs of cider in hand, bodies leaning into each other. Jabari exhaled for the first time in what felt like months. The daycare had opened. Staff were trained. Parents were satisfied. It was happening. Abike and Dana's baby was teething already.

Celeste's schedule was filling up, too. Weddings. Styled photo shoots. She had even enrolled in a business course at CPCC after her talk with Abike. Watching each other thrive made the attraction intense. The intimacy deeper. The partnership undeniable.

On their last night in the mountains, after a soft, unhurried round of lovemaking, they lay tangled beneath a thick quilt, limbs warm and bare.

Jabari kissed Celeste's shoulder, her voice hushed in the dark.

"I don't want just to love you. I want to *build* with you."

Celeste rolled to face her, brushing fingers along Jabari's collarbone. "Then let's keep building."

They talked for hours. About goals. About money. About their dreams.

Jabari confessed she had a meeting lined up with someone from the hospital network, exploring the possibility of a hospital-based employee daycare to help nurses and staff. She also wanted to open another community daycare center in an underserved neighborhood, eventually creating a network of community-rooted child development centers.

Celeste lit up as she listened. She was so proud of Jabari.

Celeste had also been busy. She'd already been tapped to style two full wedding parties, and she was working on a collaboration with a local photographer. Her brand was taking off.

"We need a regular date night," Jabari said. "Something that belongs just to us."

"Every Friday," Celeste replied. "No clients. No clipboard. Just you and me."

They lay quietly after that, hands clasped, toes brushing. Celeste shifted, her voice barely above a whisper.

"When do we start a family, babe?"

Jabari turned to her, lips parting in a slow smile. "I want kids. I'd start tomorrow if we were ready. But I also want us to be stable, financially and emotionally. I want children, though. I don't want to miss our lives because we're too busy building our professions."

"Same," Celeste said. "Let's stabilize first. Stack our money. Maybe look at buying a house. Fertility stuff isn't cheap."

Jabari nodded. "I've been thinking... what if we moved in together? We spend most of our time together anyway. Plus, we could save on rent, utilities, and gas."

Celeste grinned, "So this is your slick little way of asking me to move in with you?"

"Yes, love," Jabari said, chuckling. "But maybe we can look for something together. You need more space for your hair and makeup tools. Besides, your hair mannequin, Aniya, is always staring at me."

"You don't like Aniya?"

"She stares at me, Celeste. It's creepy."

Celeste laughed so hard she nearly fell off the bed. "She just wants love, too! You're just jealous because she has been with me since beauty school."

They settled again, giggling into each other's skin. But the next words came quietly, deliberately.

"Do you want to carry a baby?" Jabari asked.

Celeste went still.

"I don't know," she said. "It wasn't something I ever saw for myself. But with you, for our family,... I do imagine it. I want to kiss your pregnant belly. I want to feel our baby move under your skin. But I also want to feel it for myself...maybe. Just not yet."

"No pressure," Jabari murmured. "We'll figure it out together. All of it."

Celeste kissed her shoulder, then her jaw. "Hey... what would you think about commitment tattoos?"

Jabari blinked. "Okay, *plot twist.*"

"You don't have to say yes now," Celeste added. "But rings feel... wrong for me. I don't want a ring that I must take off when I work. I want something unique to us."

Jabari thought. "I could get down with that. Long as I don't end up with a cartoon heart that says 'Hot Comb Honey.'"

"Too bad," Celeste said, laughing as she straddled her. "That's my salon name now."

Jabari grinned up at her, heart pounding with joy. "Let's find something elegant. Quiet. Us."

"We will," Celeste whispered.

She nuzzled into Jabari's neck, leaving warm kisses in her wake.

They were not growing up. They were grown…both ready to be adults. This year proved that they were each a capable black woman. Together? They were unstoppable.

And in the low light of the room in the Blue Ridge Mountains, they made love again, not hurried or hungry, but slowly, reverently, the way people do when they know they've found something authentic.

Something worth building on.

Something that started with a bad hair dye, emotional intimacy, and vulnerability.

Something that grew into compassion, laughter, and desire.

And that something turned into love.

The End. (But really, just the beginning.)

AUTHOR'S INTRODUCTION TO THE BONUS CHAPTER

Let's be real, romance doesn't have to come with a hefty price tag, but it does require intention. This bonus chapter is about that very truth. Whether you're fresh out of school, juggling bills, or just navigating a tight budget, creating meaningful, intimate moments with your partner doesn't have to break the bank.

What matters most isn't money; it's effort, thoughtfulness, and being fully present. Jabari and Celeste show us how powerful it can be to plan with care, love with intention, and build a relationship rooted in connection rather than consumerism.

Love shows up in lit candles, home-cooked meals, sweaty yoga classes, and quiet glances that say I see you. I hope this chapter reminds you that magic can live in the everyday... when it's laced with love.

—Zuri Amara

BONUS CHAPTER

Date Nights

Part One: Heat And Harmony

Jabari wanted to plan something meaningful. After the months of sweetness and support they'd shared, she was ready to create a moment that brought them even closer, something intimate, fun, and a little adventurous. She stumbled upon a special couples' tantric hot yoga class at a local wellness studio and, intrigued, called to ask questions.

"Yes, we absolutely welcome same-sex couples," the warm-voiced receptionist said. "And beginners, too. Our sessions focus on connection, trust, and breathwork. You'll love it."

Reassured, Jabari booked the class.

When she brought up the idea to Celeste that evening, the resistance was immediate.

"Hot yoga?" Celeste squinted. "Babe, we live in Charlotte. It's been ninety-eight degrees for, like, the last four weeks. Why would we want to go get hotter?"

Jabari forced a smile. "It's not just about heat. It's sensual. It's slow movement, partner poses, and connection. It's supposed to deepen intimacy."

Celeste raised an eyebrow. "All I'm picturing is spandex and flexible white girls twisting themselves into pretzels while pretending they're not in pain."

Jabari's smile faltered.

She wasn't usually one to push, but she looked Celeste in the eye and said, "I know it's outside your comfort zone. We might love it. We might hate it. But I'm asking you to try something new with me. It's just one night. Please?"

Celeste softened. She reached forward and pulled Jabari into a full-body hug. "Oh, love. I'm so sorry. I was being selfish and not thinking. I love you, and of course, I'd love to experience this with you. Please forgive me, babe."

Jabari sniffled a little, blinking back emotion. "We don't have to do it if you really don't want to… I just thought it might be fun."

"I want to try it. With you."

The class turned out to be all about connection, co-regulation, shared breath, trust falls, synchronized movements, and intentional touch. Celeste's skepticism melted away within the first fifteen minutes, especially once she caught sight of Jabari glistening with sweat in tight yoga clothes. Every position they held together sparked ideas for later. Eye contact, deep trust poses, synchronized breathing, it was sensual and affirming.

"You having a good time, Celeste?" Jabari asked, her voice hushed between poses.

Celeste grinned. "The best, babe."

Later that night, they recreated a few poses in their bedroom; naked, breath syncing, bodies aligned. What began as playful mimicry turned into a deeper, slower rhythm. Their movements were grounded; their pleasure blossomed from connection. The orgasms were so intense, they lay stunned in each other's arms, unable to speak.

"You know," Celeste finally said between pants, "I think I'm a big fan of hot tantric yoga."

Jabari giggled and kissed her shoulder. "So am I, love. So am I."

Part Two: Symphony Of Light

It was Celeste's turn to plan something magical next.

Celeste had been planning for weeks, scouring discount sites and recipe blogs like a woman on a mission. She'd been determined to craft a night that spoke Jabari's love language: thoughtfulness, ambiance, intimacy. She wanted to give Jabari something unforgettable: a night worthy of the woman who held her heart, who had stood by her through fear and forgiveness and fierce commitment. Money was tight, but magic didn't have to be expensive.

She found a Groupon for a candlelight tribute concert to Queen Charlotte at the historic Great Aunt Stella Center. Elegant, timeless, romantic. It was perfect. She taught herself how to make Pad Thai from a Thai grandmother's YouTube channel, burning the first batch and getting the hang of it on her third try. She set the table with her best thrift store dishes, polished her wine glasses, and lit tea lights from the dollar store in every corner of their apartment.

On Friday morning, she kissed Jabari's cheek and said only, "Dress to impress. We're going out after dinner."

When Jabari arrived, she was radiant. Full glam. Foundation

flawless, lashes curled to the heavens, lips a deep berry red. Her hair was swept into an elegant updo, exposing the long line of her neck. She wore a simple black dress that hugged her curves like a second skin and heels that clicked with purpose. She raised an eyebrow and grinned. "What are you up to, Celeste?"

Celeste just smiled. "Dinner first. Then you'll see."

They laughed and ate, Jabari moaning over the Pad Thai like it was a five-star meal. "Okay, Chef Cee," she said, eyes wide with pride and maybe a little lust. "You stuck your foot in that."

"What!"

"Oh, sorry, babe. You're not from the South. It means you created a wonderful dish, or as we say in the country, 'stuck your foot in it.'"

Celeste shook her head and laughed. "How in the world did that become a saying? Wait, I don't want to know. I'll just take the compliment."

Jabari kept trying to guess the surprise destination between bites, tossing out everything from a poetry slam to a jazz club. But when they stepped into the Stella Center and were greeted by the golden glow of hundreds of candles lining the pews and stage, Jabari stopped short.

Her breath caught in her throat.

"Oh..."

The space was filled with soft music and flickering warmth. The string quartet took their seats and began to play a gentle melody, regal, aching, full of soul. Celeste reached for Jabari's hand and guided her down the aisle, settling them into the center row.

"You are my queen," Celeste whispered, her lips brushing Jabari's ear.

Jabari's heart thumped. Her eyes filled. She gripped Celeste's hand and blinked back tears, overwhelmed by the effort, the grace, the thoughtfulness of it all.

They sat hand in hand as the quartet played through reimagined classics and original pieces inspired by Queen Charlotte's legacy. Jabari didn't speak. She didn't need to. The candles spoke for her. So did the tears that slid quietly down her cheek as she leaned her head against Celeste's shoulder.

Later, back in their bedroom, now lit with soft lavender candles and their speaker playing the same string version of "XO" from the concert, Celeste gently undid Jabari's hair, combing through the coils with her fingers and giving a light scalp massage. Jabari melted under Celeste's attention.

"You made me feel so loved tonight," Jabari said softly, her voice thick with emotion. "No one's ever planned something like this for me."

Celeste kissed her shoulder. "I wanted you to feel how much I see you; how much you mean to me."

They undressed slowly, reverently, as if unveiling a prayer. Celeste lay Jabari down like a blessing, kissing the arch of her foot, her calf, the inside of her thigh. She worshipped her with her mouth, her hands, her devotion.

Jabari opened like a flower in bloom, every sigh a new note in the private symphony they composed with their bodies. Their rhythm was slow, steady, lush. Not a frenzy, but a tide—pulling, retreating, pulling again.

After several screaming orgasms, Jabari pulled Celeste up, their foreheads touching. "I want you too," she whispered. "Let me love you back."

Celeste let go, let herself be held, let herself be kissed like she was precious. Jabari took her time, touching her with a kind of patient hunger, like she wanted to remember every inch of skin, every tremble, every whispered yes. They rocked together, breath and sweat and light, until they shattered in each other's arms.

Afterward, tangled in sheets and candlelight, Jabari ran a lazy finger along Celeste's spine.

"I don't know what I did to deserve you," she murmured.

Celeste turned her head, eyes shining. "You dared to believe in me when I wasn't sure I could be loved like this. That's what you did."

They lay in silence for a while, the soft notes of the quartet still playing in the background, echoing the rhythm of their joined hearts.

And for the first time in a long time, Jabari didn't feel like she was chasing love.

She was resting in it.

The End

THANK YOU

Dear Reader,

Thank you for spending time with the women of Crown & Glory.

There are thousands of books in the world, and I am honored that you chose to spend a few hours with this story and these characters.

Whether you laughed, cried, blushed, smiled, or simply found a moment of escape from the demands of everyday life, I hope this visit to Crown & Glory left you feeling a little lighter and a little more hopeful than when you arrived.

As an independent author, I rely on every purchase, recommendation, and review to continue sharing stories about Black women loving Black women, finding community, healing old wounds, and discovering extraordinary love in ordinary places.

Thank you for supporting the Crown & Glory Salon Sisterhood.

With gratitude,

Zuri Amara

ABOUT THE AUTHOR

Zuri Amara

Somewhere in Charlotte, a woman walks into Crown & Glory Natural Hair Salon carrying a burden she hasn't shared with anyone.

Maybe she's grieving. Maybe she's exhausted from taking care of everyone else. Maybe she's navigating career pressures, family responsibilities, aging parents, health challenges, or the uncertainty of starting over.

By the time she leaves, she's found friendship, community, and perhaps the beginning of something beautiful.

Zuri Amara has created the Crown and Glory sisterhood for women like you. She writes passionate love stories about Black women who refuse to settle for anything less than joy, authenticity, and extraordinary love.

Through her Crown & Glory series, Zuri writes emotionally rich, sensual women-loving-women romance novels centered on Black women finding love, healing, and belonging. Her stories celebrate Black women loving Black women while blending heartfelt intimacy, sizzling chemistry, found family, and unforgettable heroines who discover that love can arrive at any age—and often when it's least expected.

Set against the backdrop of Charlotte's beloved Crown & Glory

Natural Hair Salon, her novels are filled with women carrying real-life burdens: caregiving, grief, family obligations, demanding careers, second chances, and the everyday challenges of building a meaningful life. Yet at their heart, these are hopeful stories that remind readers that joy, connection, and extraordinary love remain possible.

Readers describe Zuri's stories as emotionally rich, deeply sensual, and surprisingly healing, blending heartfelt romance with the everyday realities of Black women's lives. Whether her characters are navigating grief, family obligations, career challenges, or second chances at love, they discover that sisterhood and community can transform lives. Readers come for the romance but stay for the sisterhood, community, laughter, friendship, and the feeling of coming home.

Because Zuri knows that sometimes the greatest love story isn't about finding the right woman.

It's finding your way back to yourself.

WILL YOU HELP ANOTHER READER DISCOVER CROWN & GLORY?

If you enjoyed this story, would you consider leaving a brief review on Amazon?

Reviews are one of the most powerful ways readers help independent authors. Even a few sentences can make a tremendous difference.

Your review helps:

♥ Other readers discover books they might enjoy

♥ Increase the visibility of Black women-loving-women romance

♥ Support independent authors and small publishers

♥ Ensure more readers can find the Crown & Glory Salon Sisterhood

You don't need to write a long review. Simply sharing what you enjoyed about the story is enough.

Thank you for helping another reader find their way to Crown & Glory.

Leave your review on Amazon today.

THE BEST COMPLIMENT YOU CAN GIVE A BOOK

Love this story?

Tell a friend.

Word-of-mouth recommendations are how the Crown & Glory Salon Sisterhood continues to grow. If a character touched your heart, a romance made you smile, or a story reminded you of someone you love, consider sharing the book with a friend, a family member, a book club, or a fellow reader.

Every recommendation helps another reader discover a community where Black women are cherished, adored, comforted, desired, devoted, and loved.

Thank you for helping the Salon Sisterhood grow.

There's always room for one more at Crown & Glory.

LOVED THIS STORY?

Return to Crown & Glory in:

Devoted: A Crown and Glory Lesbian Love Story

Meet Toni and Nia:

Toni Blake never planned to fall in love again. A Navy veteran turned natural hair stylist, Toni carries the weight of loss, duty, and caregiving on her strong, quiet shoulders. She finds solace behind the chair at Charlotte's beloved Crown and Glory Natural Hair Salon, where sisterhood lives in every curl, twist, and braid.

Nia Douglas makes magic for a living—but her own heart is running on empty. As a luxury wedding planner with a flawless track record and a mile-long to-do list, Nia's used to fixing other people's love stories, not living her own. That is, until she walks into Toni's salon with five natural-haired bridesmaids, a glam vision, and a whole lot of assumptions.

JOIN THE SALON SISTERHOOD

The story doesn't end when you turn the last page.

Become part of the Crown & Glory Salon Sisterhood and enjoy exclusive content created especially for readers who can't get enough of the women of Crown & Glory.

As a member of the Sisterhood, you'll receive:

* Official Crown & Glory Spotify playlists

* Early announcements and first access to new releases

* Behind-the-scenes notes from Zuri

* Humorous short stories featuring your favorite salon sisters

* Recipes from the famous Crown & Glory gatherings, cookouts, potlucks, and celebrations

* Bonus scenes, deleted chapters, and exclusive content

* Opportunities to join advance review teams and receive early copies of upcoming books

Whether you're here for the romance, the sisterhood, the laughter, the recipes, or the community, there's always room for one more at Crown & Glory.

Join the Salon Sisterhood

Newsletter & Blog:

https://mailchi.mp/lipseylovelegacypress.com/zuri-amara

Website & Shop:

https://zuriamara.site/

Patreon:

https://www.patreon.com/ZuriAmara

Follow Zuri on Amazon:

https://amzn.to/3EUnbt6

Thank you for supporting independent Black women-loving-women romance.

With love,

Zuri Amara

Founder, Crown & Glory Salon Sisterhood

A NOTE FROM THE PUBLISHER

We are a small, independent publishing company committed to giving our readers a positive, engaging experience. If you come across any typos, grammar errors, or formatting issues that disrupt your reading, please let us know at Hello@LipseyLoveLegacyPress.com. We correct mistakes promptly.

To receive a corrected Kindle version, delete your current download and redownload the book.

Thank you for being so supportive. It truly means the world to us.

Lipsey & Love Legacy Press, LLC